Sheila on the Mend

Krystal A. Smith

Published by Whimsical Twin Publishing, 2024.

This is a work of fiction. Similarities to real people, places, or events are entirely coincidental.

SHEILA ON THE MEND

First edition. October 15, 2024.

Copyright © 2024 Krystal A. Smith.

ISBN: 979-8227469533

Written by Krystal A. Smith.

Table of Contents

Chapter 1	1
Chapter 2	15
Chapter 3	26
Chapter 4	36
Chapter 5	43
Chapter 6	51
Chapter 7	56
Chapter 8	67
Chapter 9	82
Chapter 10	93
Chapter 11	102
Chapter 12	110
Chapter 13	117
Chapter 14	126
Chapter 15	133
Chapter 16	141
Chapter 17	150
Chapter 18	160
Chapter 19	169
Chapter 20	178
Chapter 21	187
Chapter 22	195
Chapter 23	204

Chapter 1

Sheila letting her soon to be sister-in-law talk her into going to a strip club for a pre-bachelorette party with her friends and sorors was part of her attempt at stepping out of her comfort zone. It really wasn't her thing, but they'd hyped it up so much that it actually sounded fun, and she didn't want to be the downer of the group. Since coming into her life Kelly always made an effort to include her in events and gatherings, so Sheila appreciated the invite.

Even though she didn't physically feel like being around all these people, and the noise of the club was too loud already as they stood outside the club, Sheila told herself she'd have a good time. Plus, this sounded more reasonable than the divorce party Kelly had offered to throw her.

It had been hard to even think about having a good time the last few months while waiting for things to be finalized. Her divorce from Kharla had taken her through a depth of loneliness and frustration she had never expected. With work and research and planning committees to keep herself busy she hadn't really tried to have a personal life. The natural intensity and vigor of teaching at a midsize college had given her enough to do while she rebounded.

"I'm so glad you agreed to come, Sheila. I know this isn't really your vibe." Kelly looped her arm under Sheila's and pulled her close as they waited to go in.

Sheila was about an inch taller than Kelly, but she'd worn flats tonight and Kelly's sky-high heels made it so she had to look up at her.

"I'm actually kind of excited. I always have fun with you. Your friends are so nice too. They better be prepared for lap dances. I have a purse full of singles." Sheila nudged her brother's fiancée and smiled.

They stood chatting and listening to the noise around them. It had been a long time since Sheila had had to stand in line to get in somewhere. She didn't like it. She felt too old to be standing outside with men and women half her age to get into a crowded, loud, establishment. Rolling her eyes to herself as her feet were already starting to hurt, she at least had fun getting dressed up. The blue jewel-toned asymmetrical top fit snug against her torso, showing off her soft shoulders and full breasts. The sliver of stomach the top left exposed had her questioning her choices, but the high waisted wide-leg pants she'd slipped into accentuated her hips while being comfortable. Kelly had done her makeup, lightly powdering her face to keep her almond shaped eyes and pouty lips front and center.

"Excuse me, Miss?"

Kelly nudged Sheila in the shoulder. An average height, clean-shaven Black man with a clipboard approached from the side of the line. He wore his black-on-black suit tight, showing off a firm physique. He looked bored, but pleasant standing there occasionally tapping the earpiece he wore.

"Are you ready to come inside, Miss?" His voice was even despite the other people in line reaching out to him and trying to get his attention.

"Do you know him, Sheila?"

"Who me?" Sheila was surprised anyone even noticed her standing there. She'd never been to this strip club before or any strip club for that matter and was surprised this man had approached.

"Yes, you. I've been told to move you to the front of the line."

"I-I..." She stammered and looked from left to right. "I'm with my friends. Kelly here is the bachelorette."

"Absolutely. You and your friends can come right in."

"You little minx!" Kelly whispered in Sheila's ear. "You're a VIP!"

The other women cheered, flaunting a bit of superiority towards the other patrons before gathering around Sheila, who had no idea why they were being treated to a special escort inside. She wondered who they were being mistaken for and hoped this didn't turn out to be an embarrassing or costly mistake.

"I do not know why they are letting us skip the line. This is so bizarre."

"This is *fabulous!* Don't question it!" One of Kelly's sorors, Brie, flicked her shimmering black hair over her shoulder and pushed out her chest. "This should happen to beautiful women such as us everywhere we go."

"Amen to that!"

One by one the ladies followed the clipboard man into the club to the roped off VIP area. Shimmering lights splashed glitter illusion all around on the walls, the floor, and into the crowd on the floor. VIP was furnished with navy and plum plush couches covered in velvet. The angle of the booth was such that anyone inside could see out onto the floor, but looking in only granted a view of the partitions. Sheila, Kelly, Brie and the two other women, Sophia and Deana, sat down as three beautiful muscular dancers walked over.

"Welcome, ladies! We heard there is a bride-to-be over here."

"Right here!" They pointed to Kelly.

"Congratulations!" Two of the dancers pulled her to the center of the floor area and danced on her while the third woman grabbed a chair. "We've got a little show for you."

Sheila squealed and put her hands up to her face. She had a very clear concept of strip clubs, but it was a different thing to see attractive women in barely there garments simulating sex on her brother's fiancée. It was scintillating as much as she hated to admit it. She couldn't understand why she was blushing so hard. As a fully grown woman who was no stranger to enticement, and who loved making love with women, she shouldn't have been so astonished.

Brie slid over to sit beside Sheila as a full-figured dancer demonstrated her flexibility in front of them. "Kelly said you'd never been to a strip club before. How are you doing?"

"I didn't expect to be so...*aroused*." Sheila covered her face and laughed. She needed to calm down and relax.

"It's hot, right?"

"Definitely that." Sheila looked up at the long partition needing to disrupt the intense visual stimulation, but the embedded monitors displayed more women dancing and gyrating to music she couldn't hear. This was the most *action* she'd been privy to in ages since even before her divorce. Sheila shook her head and turned her attention back to the three thick-thighed beauties dancing on Kelly. She hadn't meant to think of the divorce or Kharla or the empty bed she'd return to tonight. She cleared her throat, looked to the others as they danced in their seats, and spoke over the din of music. "Who's ready for shots?"

"SHOTS! SHOTS! SHOTS!" They all sang in unison and Sheila waived over one of the servers. She ordered for the group. As the mahogany beauty walked away to put in their drink orders, another woman approached the VIP area. This one wore a designer suit in deep mulberry with a black crew neck. The lights bounced off her simple necklace and white teeth. She looked like a boss, a young boss sporting a tapered fade with the sharpest of edges. A few long curls on the top of her head fell across her face, adding to a mysterious sex appeal.

Sheila found her even more attractive than the half-naked women dancing before her. It was the way she moved. Like she owned the place, like nothing could touch her.

Ladies! Welcome to The Lounge. I'm Cy, club owner. Are you having a good time?"

"Yes!" The response came in unison.

"I won't keep you from your celebration. I hope you have a titillating time tonight." She turned her attention to Sheila, tilting her head a bit. "Dr. Hudson?"

Sheila raised her eyebrows. How on earth did this fine specimen know her name? "Y-yes?" Sheila felt a sudden rush of heat rise up her neck.

"Dr. Sheila Hudson. I thought that was you. I was fortunate enough to take a couple of your seminars at Mill-Amherst. You did a queer literature series that was quite amazing. I still think about it to this day." Cy had subtly closed the space between them and her deep woodsy warm scent mixed with a hint of body sweat engulfed Sheila, sending her arousal to another level.

Sheila pulled her thoughts back to the conversation acknowledging Cy. "That's incredible. So, you're a student of literature then?"

"Unfortunately, no." She chuckled. "My folks were adamant I get a business degree, but I absolutely love reading. Your lectures spurred some intense conversations among my friends and I."

"I appreciate you saying that."

The server with the shots appeared along with a couple of bottle girls carrying champagne and a glass for Cy.

"And if it's not inappropriate I have to admit I had the biggest crush on you." Cy sipped from her glass without taking her eyes off Sheila.

Sheila, surprised for what felt like the umpteenth time that night, emptied her shot glass and then took a sip of champagne without lowering her eyes. She could hold a gaze just as well.

"Is that right?" She fingered the rim of the glass in her hand while she tried to gauge if she looked crush worthy still. "Well," she paused and took a longer sip from her glass, "I'm flattered."

"Woo, Professor!" Kelly and the other girls shouted encouraging and inappropriate suggestions for her and Cy to hear. They easily listened to the exchange while continuing to dance and drink.

"I'd really enjoy getting together with you sometime to talk about...anything." Cy took out a business card, then a pen, and scribbled on the back of it. "Will you call me?"

The warmth of the shots and champagne were swirling up to Sheila's cheeks and she felt the initial tingle of alcohol attack her system. She took the business card and nodded. She was struggling to maintain eye contact this time.

"Wonderful." Cy then addressed the group. "If you ladies need anything tonight, anything at all, don't hesitate to let my staff or myself know."

"Thank you."

"Yes, thank you," Kelly shouted. She had stepped away from the dancers to listen to Sheila and Cy's conversation more intently. She waved as Cy walked away and once she disappeared among the patrons on the main floor Kelly squealed. "Okay, Professor! Dr. Sheila Hudson got that sex appeal."

"Oh, stop it! She was just being nice."

"Well, either way she is good looking and looking at you!" Kelly lifted her glass up to one of the cameras above the VIP section.

Sheila let the ridiculousness of the idea wash over her and leaned into Kelly's swaying movement. For the rest of the night she danced and ordered drinks while wagging dollar bills at beautiful women.

For the first time in months she felt a little lighter, a little sexier. Nothing like flirting to lift the recently divorced blues.

• • • •

"Ladies, it's about that time," Sheila said, pointing to her watch. She'd been watching the clock like a hawk after midnight. Tired and more tipsy than she'd planned to be, Sheila was ready to get home and take her shoes off.

"Excuse me, I need to settle up. I'm taking care of all the drinks."

The server smiled. "Everything has already been taken care of by the owner."

"What? Are you sure?"

"Absolutely. Y'all have a good night." The server walked away without protest, leaving Sheila a bit stunned.

"Did you have a good time tonight?" Brie slipped her left breast back into her bra.

"What happened to you?"

Brie shrugged and smiled.

"What happens at the club stays at the club. Got it." Despite the alcohol coursing through her system Sheila caught on quickly.

Just then Kelly approached with the other two women, Sophia and Deana. "This was just what I needed. I'm so glad y'all came tonight. Best girls' night ever."

"Is everyone ready?"

Sophia, Deana, and Brie took a car service to the Crest Heights area where they all lived within a few blocks of each other. Sheila and Kelly shared a car to Mt. Mullon. After dropping Kelly off, Sheila reclined in the backseat replaying her interaction with Cy. She was attractive. Deep brown eyes with thick lashes, full kissable lips, and squarish jaw. Her voice was rich. That had always been one of Sheila's favorite features. A melodic voice on the deeper side. Kharla had a rich, low register and a booming laugh that had always sent shivers up and down Sheila's spine. She missed having someone to make her laugh and to talk to and snuggle next to in bed. The warmth, the comfort...It had gone missing in their marriage after Kharla's career change from hospitality to private sector tech, but she'd never imagined it would stay gone.

The car service stopped in front of her house and she promptly got out, hurrying up the short walkway. She hadn't been out until 3am since she was a student in college the first time. Sheila felt a little giddy as she unlocked the door and removed her jacket. She still wasn't quite used to this new house and took her time walking around the furniture in the dark. There was a light switch somewhere on the front wall, but after sliding her hand around for a few seconds she decided she could manage in the dark. The shoes were the first things to come off before she traipsed down the hall. The closer she got to the bedroom the more tired and heavy she felt. She'd shower in the morning. Right now she needed a glass of water, two aspirin, and to fall into bed. Thank goodness tomorrow was Sunday. She would sleep in and relax before going over her research notes and summer strategy.

Sheila slipped out of her clothes and left them where they fell. The sheets were calling but she needed to wash her face.

The light in the bathroom was harsh. She'd forgotten, again, to order the soft amber lights that gave everything a warm tone like the cozy custom lights in the bathroom she and Kharla had picked out when they built what was to be their forever home.

Now she was scrubbing eyeliner off in this new place separate from what she'd known for the last seven years.

"Loving ain't easy," Sheila started to sing until her voice cracked and she sighed. She flicked off the bathroom light and carried her water cup to the bedside table.

The sheets were cold. Chill bumps sprouted across her thighs reviving an ache between her legs that had been simmering for months but that she'd been too preoccupied to really acknowledge. Tonight, she wouldn't ignore it. She reached into the top drawer of the bedside table retrieving Sappho, her vibrator, and settled back into the sheets. The buzz of the powerful apparatus quieted as soon as she slipped it under the covers. And just as she closed her eyes to concentrate Sheila fell asleep.

• • • •

In the morning Sheila woke up groggy, with a slight headache behind one eye. The buzzing she thought was in her head was her vibrator knocking against the headboard. It had shimmied its way up the bed and nestled in the space between the mattress and headboard. She flicked the off switch and tossed it back in the nightstand drawer. So much for taking that edge off. Sheila sat up in bed with her feet dangling just above the floor for quite a while. She wasn't ready to get up, but she had things to do even though it was Sunday. There were still a couple of boxes she hadn't yet unpacked, and she was sure her favorite shorts were tucked away in one of them. She vowed to get through her chores quickly so she could relax and catch up on her guilty pleasure show *Rosa, Rosa!* a telenovela her college roommate got her hooked on when they were sophomores. A glass or two of wine, and several episodes would get her ready for the week.

After a long, hot shower and dressing for some casual work and lounging around the house Sheila took her blood pressure medicine, then immediately stripped the linens from the bed. For breakfast she made a creamy bowl of oatmeal topped with berries and a foamy decaf latte with the espresso machine her dad conveniently found still in the box when she'd announced her separation from Kharla over fourteen months ago. Braxton Hudson wasn't much on words, but he was the type of man who always wanted his kids to know he was there for them. Sheila smiled thinking about him and made a mental note to call him later in the day. She made a list of other things she wanted to get done while standing at the kitchen counter when she remembered she had just tossed her jacket and clutch toward the couch when she'd gotten home last night. The jacket was probably wrinkled, and all the contents of her bag were likely spilled and lost within the crevices of the couch cushions.

Sheila grabbed her latte and went to survey the damage. The house was different from what she had been accustomed to on two incomes, but it was cozy and eclectic. Her dad called it bungalow chic and had built her some additional storage off the master bedroom for all her seasonal items and accessories.

Neither the jacket nor the clutch had found its way to the couch. Crumpled on the floor beside the coffee table, the jacket looked like a nest for a small creature and the clutch hadn't fared much better. The clasp on the clutch had to have given up containing the contents of the purse as soon as it hit the floor. Sheila squatted down, her right knee squeaking in protest, and gathered the lip gloss, makeup brush, and cards that had spread across the floor. The clasp had indeed snapped on one side, leaving just a ragged edge where the two balls should have met, and the metal frame bent. She ran her finger over it. Maybe it could be replaced. This was one of her favorite little going out bags. The right size for essentials and tucking under her arm. She turned her attention back to corralling the loose items all over the floor. She put her fingernail on a little triangle of white poking out from the edge of the rug.

In giant squiggly letters across the top was The LOUNGE. She flipped it over in her hand. *Cy - 570-821-9494.*

She hadn't dreamed it. A good-looking, club-owning, past attendee of one of her lectures had given her a card with their number on it and flirted with her. The same tingling excitement from last night spread all over her body and Sheila felt *joy,* and something else, move through her. It was definitely nice to still be seen as an attractive person at her age. She looked good for a fifty something but hadn't felt her best in years and with the divorce just barely under her belt feeling good, felt great.

She wasn't going to call Cy, probably. The owner had to be at least twenty years younger than Sheila and she was probably only being nice, asking her to get together *to talk.* Cy said she'd *had* a crush, not that she maintained one currently. Besides, in her mind it was too soon to be entertaining women. Although physical affection was higher up on her list of needs than she liked to admit. Sheila tucked the card back into her purse and set everything in their proper places right before moving on to her to-do list.

• • • •

When Kelly called later in the evening, they chatted and laughed and talked about Kelly's upcoming wedding.

"I love my brother, but you could do better, Kelly."

"Stop. Bryce is a good man. He treats me better than I've ever known."

"That's all good and fine, Kelly, but have you seen his feet?" Sheila made a gagging noise.

"I'm telling him you said that," Kelly said, trying to quell her laughter.

"Please do. Maybe he'll go with you to get a pedicure sometime. Those claws are prehistoric."

"You're so bad. Let me get off this phone before he comes in here and wants to know why I'm giggling so hard."

"Okay. Talk to you soon."

"Bye."

Sheila looked at the lock screen of her phone and saw what time it was. Dinner time had come and gone, and she hadn't even noticed. Her appetite had whittled away to nothing during the separation and all the back and forth with the lawyers. She was hungry tonight though. There was some chicken and things in the fridge, but Sheila didn't have the best track record with cooking. That had been Kharla's department. Her ex-wife knew more things to do with thyme and rosemary than Sheila could ever start to imagine.

SHEILA ON THE MEND

Sheila unlocked her phone and opened a delivery app, *Quickies*. It had everything at the touch of a button: Cajun, home style, Italian, you name it. This was how she liked to "cook". With options at her fingertips and hardly having to lift a finger. She scrolled through until she found Tikka Hut, terrible name, but the best Indian food in all of the northeast. She added several dishes to her order and pressed the button. It would arrive in thirty minutes and her kitchen would remain clean. That was the part that she truly frowned upon. The cleaning up afterward.

While she waited for her food she started an episode of *Rosa, Rosa!* While her spanish was conversational, Sheila knew she missed quite a bit of subtext, so she put the subtitles on and reclined and stretched out on the couch. Her thoughts wandered back and forth between the show and Kharla. She couldn't help wondering what she might be doing tonight. That irritated her because she knew Kharla wasn't thinking about her or her feelings or...

The doorbell rang and Sheila was happy to get up and get her food. "Thank you!" She waved to the delivery person's back as they walked away. The aroma of garlic naan and chicken tikka masala wafted up out of the giant sack. Sheila set her delicacies on the coffee table and restarted the episode of *Rosa, Rosa!* again. She was determined to enjoy the rest of the evening with no more wayward thoughts of Kharla.

After three episodes and a mountain of basmati, Sheila found herself sprawled across the couch, rubbing her stomach. She drifted in and out of a light sleep, with blurry images of the past and present mixing.

Images of Kharla and the house they'd shared. Trips and vacations where she'd felt loved and cared for blurred with arguments and phone calls with the lawyers. Her new home and all the adjustments she'd had to make were aloft in the background.

She was wandering around in a space she didn't know, growing more frustrated every time she entered a room, and it wasn't what she expected. Sheila tossed on the couch until she woke herself up. Remnants of her dream still floating around in her head. She looked around the room confirming she was alone.

Chapter 2

Monday morning Sheila woke up refreshed. Warm light shone through the bedroom windows and Sheila rolled over into where it splashed across the bed. She liked being able to sprawl out across the expensive sheets she'd picked out without worrying about disturbing anyone. And she'd been dreaming more. Or at least remembering them. She'd been holding hands with someone in her dreams last night and laughing. Feeling extremely light and relaxed. That feeling carried through to the morning and she felt as if she had a new attitude altogether.

After a few more minutes reveling in the warm sun covered sheets, Sheila shot up remembering her summer break had officially started. She was determined to make the most of her time away from the college in order to work on her research. The excitement built as she quickly ran through a mental list of what she needed to do. She needed to buy supplies and that meant she could go to the fancy stationery store near her favorite coffee shop downtown.

"I love research," she said, springing out of bed.

It was a perfect summer day as she maneuvered in and out of traffic driving to the quaint shopping center. The breeze, the bright green in the leaves, and the warmth in the air added to her feeling of relaxed renewal. She was looking forward to walking around with the sun caressing her skin.

Sheila made her way over to the coffee shop for a latte and pastry. She wanted to make her supplies list before she went over to the stationery store. As excited as she was, her tendency to lose control at the sight of crisp notepads, pens, and highlighters could bust her budget wide open. She had to save something for the copy machines on campus.

As soon as she stepped into the coffee shop the smell of roasting coffee and fresh baked goods took over her senses.

"Welcome to Sheeva's. Good morning."

"Good morning." Sheila bent toward the pastry case eyeing the glistening cinnamon rolls on the top shelf before stepping up to order. "I have to have a cinnamon roll. They look delicious."

"They are. Good choice." The cashier looked like she could be a student. Her ponytail bobbed as she nodded. "Would you like a coffee or tea to go with your pastry?"

"Yes, I'll have a half caf coconut latte too." Sheila paid and moved down to the end of the counter. When she did, she spotted a familiar face from Mill-Amherst.

"Darcy!" Dr. Frasier was one of the other Black women in Sheila's department. They often shared "the look" during faculty meetings when someone said something unhinged or borderline unforgivable. Sheila had greatly valued her friendship since she'd come to Mill-Amherst.

"Sheila, hi!"

Darcy sauntered over like she was in a music video. Her glossy hair flowed behind her with the invisible wind that seemed to always be with her. Darcy often joked she had *Big Dick Energy*, and no one could get in her way.

"Fancy meeting you here." They shared a brief embrace.

"I can't resist their orange scones, girl. I was going to park it at a table and get some reading and syllabus work done. My office is too quiet at the beginning of the summer semester."

"Oh, I know." Sheila waited as Darcy added cream and sweetener to her coffee before grabbing a table. The coffee shop was getting busier, so they navigated their way through the growing crowd and found a spot near the windows. "I almost got roped into teaching two classes, but with everything I've been through recently I wanted to actually enjoy my summer. I'm stocking up on supplies, then I might head over to the campus research library."

"That sounds perfect to be honest. I know you're still dealing with the aftermath of *Miss Thing*." Sheila laughed. Despite being adamant about not wanting to harbor hard feelings on her side over the divorce, Sheila deeply appreciated how Darcy refused to call Kharla by name. The act of solidarity felt really nice.

"It is, isn't it? I love the students, but I do need a break from that pace. Just thinking about hunting down old books and reading interviews and case studies makes me giddy." Sheila felt the smile stretch to her eyes.

"You are such a nerd!" Darcy playfully rolled her eyes and sipped her coffee. "And I'm jealous. I've hardly had any time to write or read anything other than weirdly written freshmen and sophomore essays."

"It'll level out. Don't even think about getting overwhelmed."

They sat in companionable silence listening to the other patrons and the usual sounds of a coffee shop while they themselves worked. Sheila made her supplies list, a to-do for the week, and various notes for her trip to the library. Darcy sent a couple of emails from her computer and drafted course documents until her phone rang and she excused herself from the table.

"My husband is just goofy sometimes," she said upon return. "This man thought the entire crock pot went in the dishwasher." She closed her eyes and pulled a deep breath through her nose.

"Bless it."

"He's seen me pull that ceramic body out of the stand five thousand times." Darcy rolled her eyes then turned her attention back to her computer.

"Hey, your husband is younger than you, right?"

"Mmhm. Just a few years though."

"How many is a few," Sheila asked. Her mind had gone to her brief interaction with Cy Saturday night.

"He's five years younger than me. We are in the same generation. He should know better than putting shit with electrical cords in the dishwasher."

Sheila laughed and nodded but continued on her line of questioning. "What's too old of an age gap, do you think? Ten? Twenty years?"

"I guess it depends on the people. I couldn't date a twenty-something. That's our students, you know. But a thirsty thirty-something could get it." Darcy smirked and looked off as if she had someone in mind.

Sheila played with the ends of her hair; the graduated bob made her feel like Taraji P. Henson. The perfect cut for a sexy summer. Her thoughts continued to drift off with images of her galivanting around before being interrupted by Darcy's curiosity.

"Looks like you're asking for a reason. Who's studying you? Cos these young ones will shoot their shot in a heartbeat."

Sheila couldn't contain the smile spreading across her face. Darcy was right. The boldness was shocking, and sexy, exactly what she needed to clear the cobwebs and doubt in her kind.

"Must be someone real cute if you're smiling and grinning over there like *How Stella Got Her Groove Back*."

They both threw their heads back with laughter drawing the attention of the two tables to their right.

"Cheers to that." Sheila raised her cup and Darcy bumped her mug to it.

"Do you think...it's too soon to date? I've definitely got some things to work out. But is there a timeframe?"

"Hell no. You deserve fun and romance and S.E.X!"

"During this whole separation and divorce process I've realized I was kind of only married on paper. I don't even think Kharla and I still liked each other." Sheila sighed. The realization hit harder once she'd said it out loud. If she started up a new romance, hell, even a fling, she wanted to like the person she was with. She wanted to be able to talk about all aspects of their days and even argue with respect.

After an hour of planning at the coffee shop, Sheila had the rest of her day worked out and left Darcy to her work in the coffee shop. Sheila wanted to ask Darcy more questions about dating younger, but that would have to wait for another day. Sheila made her way to the stationery store down the block.

You Write About That! was the cutest little store. It was one of her favorite places when she'd moved to the house close to the college. When she couldn't get out of her feelings over separating from Kharla, then finalizing the divorce, she'd come and get fancy paper and folders and sparkling paper clips.

As soon as she walked in she was smiling. Her eyes went wide as she looked around. There were new displays for summer that she would definitely check out. She could see the *Professional Series* section at the back of the store and her pulse picked up. But before she walked back to her favorite section she stepped up to the counter and gently hit the bell.

"Welcome to You Write About That. I'll be right there." The disembodied voice floated from the open storeroom. "I'm tangled in ribbon," the voice continued as she approached the front.

"Gail, it's me, Sheila."

"Sheila, what a pleasant surprise. How are you?" Gail stumbled forward. She had cellophane clinging to her feet and a spool of purple specialty ribbon trailing behind her. "I don't know how I did this to myself." Her voice held a light airy lift to it. She was always so upbeat and happy.

"Here let me help." Sheila grabbed the loose spool of ribbon from the floor and rewound it. She released Gail from her shackles and further cleared other tripping hazards.

"Saved by the professor."

"I got here at just the right time it seems."

"Yes, you did. Inventory was about to take me out. Are you gearing up for summer classes?" She frowned, then smiled. "Summer always makes me both happy and a little sad." Gail set two boxes on the counter to unpack alongside a hand size label and pricing machine.

Sheila leaned on the counter. This is why she liked Gail's store and Gail too. She wasn't just a businesswoman; she was personable and cared about her customers and the community too. They'd run into each other at several community events.

"Nope, I got a little funding for my research this summer. I can finally get started on a project I've been putting off for years. Which is what brings me in today. Breaking in my budget with some quality supplies."

"How exciting indeed!"

SHEILA ON THE MEND

Gail reached across the counter with a gentle hand and squeezed Sheila's arm. "Let's hope I've got all the things on your list."

"How do you know I have a list?"

Gail tilted her head and smirked. "You are the epitome of organized beauty. You absolutely have a list."

Sheila snorted then quickly covered her mouth. Gail wasn't wrong. She opened her cherry-colored leather portfolio and pulled out her meticulously written list.

"This is going to be fun."

"Yeah, it is," Sheila agreed.

Gail had the brilliant idea to split the list. She made a copy and took responsibility for the bottom half while Sheila took the top.

For research Sheila had a system of cataloging data. Interviews, readings, and media all needed color coding. So, she needed folders, preferably accordion with interchangeable label tags. She needed pens, highlighters, pencils with extremely strong erasers and paper. Oh, how she needed paper! Not just one kind of paper either. There were levels to this. Notebooks, notepads, index cards, post-its, and transparent vellum for diagrams if Gail had it.

Sheila walked through the store just giddy and smiling as she grabbed items and marked them off her list one by one. She didn't know why these things excited her, they just did, and she reveled in having something so simple but pleasing. She'd let Kharla tag along once for her research supply gathering and she bitched the entire time. Complaining and suggesting what she thought would be much more useful digital items, not understanding why Sheila insisted on folders and such. It had caused a fight and, if she recalled, Kharla slept elsewhere that night.

Before Sheila could dwell on that old memory, Gail popped out of the backroom with her half of the list checked off and a smile on her face.

"How's your hunt going?"

"Oh, I don't know why I love this so much. I've found everything and then some. How about you?"

"I've got everything, including the vellum. I also have a heavier weight that the art students seem to really enjoy so I brought up a box for you to look at." Gail set the items on the counter approval.

Sheila got quiet as she gently opened one end of the box and stroked her finger over the paper. It was cool to the touch and silky. It smelled slightly of mint and artificial air. Sheila closed her eyes for just a second.

"I brought my ex-wife with me last time and she ruined it for me. She didn't get why I wanted what I wanted for my last research project. She was downright mean about it. I'm replacing that moment with this one."

Sheila pushed her shoulders up and back and handed over her Amex to Gail who simply nodded.

Sheila made two trips to the car to pack in her supplies. She had one more task before she needed to go to campus. At one time there had been an antique shop in one of the buildings along the same street as *You Write About That*. She was hoping they could look at the broken clasp on her purse and tell her if it was fixable. It was one of those old-timey baubles cast in metal. She started across the street but before she could reach the sidewalk she stopped, completely caught off guard by the sight of Cy walking out of the jewelry store. She was dressed in dark green floral print trousers and a cream striped top. Her skin was more golden bronze in the daylight opposed to the cool brown of the nightclub. Her long stride made her appear relaxed and confident which sent a shiver up Sheila's spine. She carried several small shopping bags and had an accomplished look on her face.

Sheila allowed herself to imagine walking beside Cy and carrying on playful conversation when a car slammed on its brakes in the middle of the road to avoid hitting her.

"Hey! What are you doing?" The driver laid on the horn and gestured out the driver's side window. Sheila stepped quickly out of the road, raising her hand in apology. She'd allowed herself to drift in thought and almost got smooshed in the process. She touched her hand to her chest as if checking to see if her heart was still there, unaware that Cy had witnessed the incident and was approaching.

"Are you alright? At least they stopped."

"Yeah, I was being careless—" Sheila turned around and as soon as she was inches away from Cy's deep brown eyes, she felt her chest tighten. Lightheaded and unsteady, Sheila reached out and Cy responded.

"Easy, easy. I gotcha."

The full weight of her embarrassment hit, and Sheila found herself without words. She looked down at the ground hoping to find some composure or a crack wide enough for her to fall through. She stared at Cy's shiny black shoes slowly trying to coax air back through her lungs. "Okay, I think I'm okay now."

Sheila noticed Cy still held her lightly by the elbow. If she concentrated on that spot, she might get lightheaded again. "Hi again." She had to do something to break the connection with that touch.

"Hello, Dr. Hudson."

"Sheila. Please call me Sheila."

"Okay, Sheila. I didn't think I'd see you again so soon." Cy maneuvered so she was closest to the street. She guided Sheila toward the shops, and they fell into step, side by side.

"I was running some errands. Do you shop in this area often?"

"Not too often. I was grabbing a few gifts." She indicated the two bags in her left hand. "My mom's birthday is in two days. We go all out. She loves gifts so we kinda spoil her."

"That's so sweet." Sheila thought about her own mom who didn't particularly care to have a fuss made over her unless no one took the initiative to do so. Then they were all disrespectful and undeserving of her attention. "Are you having a party?"

"Just a little get together. Not too many people."

Sheila nodded. She was once again letting the connection and ease of their simple conversation take her over. Cy smelled good too and that had always been a quick path to Sheila's attraction. Sweet, earthy, woodsy notes traveled up her nose and straight to the part of her brain that said, *Yes!*

"Do you think you'd have time to get together later this week?" The words were coming out of her mouth with such casual flow, like she was scheduling a meeting.

Cy didn't try hiding her smile. "I'll be honest, I didn't think for two seconds you'd call me."

"But you gave me your number anyway?"

"I'm not shy. Never have been."

"Well, that makes me the lucky one, huh?" Sheila averted her eyes. She wasn't sure she was even doing the right thing. But it seemed more than just coincidental that she happened to run into this woman so soon after meeting her. "Friday?"

"Yeah, yeah, Friday."

"Okay." Sheila felt herself warming all over. The noon church bells a couple streets over filled the air with historic song and Sheila looked at her watch. "Oh, shoot, I have to run." Sheila looked toward the street.

Cy took the initiative to walk with her to her car, lest she freeze up again and encounter another impatient motorist in the roadway.

"I'll call you to confirm, yeah?" Sheila stood by the open car door.

"Please do."

Sheila glanced in the rearview a couple times as she pulled out of the parking lot.

Cy stood there waiting for a few seconds then walked back across the street to continue her shopping. Half a mile down the road Sheila realized she was driving in the wrong direction. She needed to go to campus, not home. She laughed at herself and wondered who that was back there initiating a date and smiling despite herself.

There was a new version of her emerging from the old and it was both unsettling and encouraging.

Chapter 3

On Wednesday Sheila did call Cy to confirm their date. It was early afternoon after a morning in the research library on campus when Sheila took a break outside on one of the benches near the coffee cart.

"Cy? Hi, this is Sheila. How are you?"

"Better now. One hundred percent."

"Glad to hear it. Well, I wanted to make sure you were still up for our...*date* Friday. I was thinking we could check out the new exhibit at the museum and then have dinner."

"The Warrior Women exhibit?"

"Oh, no, have you already been?" Sheila was quickly trying to think of something else they could do.

"No, but I've been wanting to go. That sounds perfect."

"Oh, good. I hear it's fantastic. I think we'll enjoy it."

"Definitely." Cy sounded genuinely excited.

"And lastly is there anything you're in the mood for food wise?"

Cy cleared her throat. "I have to say, I'm not used to this type of initiative. I like it."

"I take it you usually do the asking, huh?" Sheila chuckled into the phone. She was a bit entertained by the way this was turning out.

"I hope you don't think I'm some sort of player type. Owning a strip club seems to make people think about me in a certain way."

"I've not had too much time to do a great deal of thinking about you yet." Sheila was grinning and nibbling at her lip. Where this flirtatious tone came from, she didn't know, but she liked the way her voice sounded.

"You're right about that." It was Cy's turn to laugh. She answered the question Sheila had asked about food, indicating there were a couple restaurants near the museum she absolutely loved.

"Okay. I'll make arrangements for us."

"I could get used to this."

"Listen, I believe in fair play, ok. You don't have to do all the heavy lifting."

"Oooh, but I will," Cy teased. "I have no problem with doing my part."

Sheila smiled into the phone until she realized the silence had gone on a bit too long. "Okay, well, I can't wait to see you. I'll meet you at the museum at seven."

"Sounds good. I'll see you then."

Sheila remained at the bench looking at her phone. She wasn't sure if she was doing the right thing, but something about the way she felt just being in communication with Cy was a welcome change to her life right now.

She had an hour left before the microfiche room closed for the evening and she wanted to search for an article that predated most of her known sources. As she got up to go back inside, she got a text from her brother.

Don't forget dinner at ours tonight. Sevenish.

Sheila sent a thumbs up emoji back, then proceeded back into the library. She made her way down to the lower level where the periodicals and study carrels were located. She'd left her materials in one of the carrels while she'd been using the microfiche machine.

"Dr. Hudson?"

Sheila spun around to see who called her name. "Remi, hi. How are you?" It was one of her students from last semester. She pushed a cart full of books in front of her as she restocked the shelves.

"I'm great. Excited for this summer."

"Good. What are you taking?"

Remi closed one eye to recall her classes. "Econ, Literature of the Renaissance, and then work study. Working down here feels like such a cheat code. I was able to get some of my books for class just by checking them out."

"Very nice. I know how expensive it can be."

"Are you teaching at all this summer? I wanted to take one of your classes again."

"I'm doing research this term. Hopefully I can make something of it."

"I'm sure you will. Let me know if you need anything. I can recall books and process interlibrary loans. I got your back, Dr. H."

"Nice. I'll keep that in mind."

Sheila let her student get back to work. She liked being able to interact with the student community in and out of the classroom. Rumor on campus was that she was a cool professor. Sheila smiled and went back to search the microfiche. She was having trouble finding what she was looking for and, because her eyes were starting to lose focus, she decided she needed to call it a day to regroup. Her phone chimed while she gathered her items from the study carrel. Assuming her brother was leaving another message about dinner she ignored it until she was back at her car. To Sheila's surprise it was Kharla who had texted.

Need to see you. It's important.

Important issues go through the lawyer.
It's better that way.

SHEILA ON THE MEND

Really, Sheila? You're being childish.
Just meet me at my parents' house in thirty minutes.

No.

Sheila dropped her phone in the passenger seat and took a deep breath. A mix of anger and frustration bubbled up inside her as her phone continued to chime.

Through all the back and forth of the separation and divorce, lawyers, paralegals, and assistants she knew to be all up in her business, and the stress of her relationship transitioning to nothing, Sheila had gotten through it all by telling herself she wouldn't have to deal with Kharla's moods, attitude, and demands anymore. It was just another letdown for her to have to navigate. Sheila picked her phone back up to block Kharla, but noticed not only she was texting, but her ex-mother-in-law had sent a couple messages too.

Sheila it's momma Joyce. I sure do miss
hearing from you. You can still come by
the house and speak if you'd like.
Me and John still love you. Kharla
needs your help with those boxes
in the back and she wants to
talk to you, hon. Just stop by okay.

Was this the way Kharla was going to play it from now on? Instead of leaving Sheila to her peace Kharla was going to order her to appear and use her mother to guilt her into being in contact.

It didn't seem fair. None of it did. The entire uprooting of her life as she knew it, the act of starting over as a fifty-two-year-old woman. What had she done to deserve any of this? Sheila waited until she thought she could safely drive home before starting the car and navigating the library parking lot. Her plan for the night was to soak in the tub and take as much time as she needed to get ready for dinner with Bryce and Kelly. She didn't think she could take any more surprises today.

Her feelings had hardly dissipated by the time she got home. Walking through the door served as another pinch of salt in the wound of her life, but Sheila felt a little relief after she slammed the door. She refused to let the tornado of feelings fester inside her the way she'd done throughout her marriage. Even if that meant taking it out on the existing furniture and items around her.

Crossing the living room into the open kitchen, she grabbed a glass from the cabinet and slammed that door shut too. Opening the cabinet a second time she slammed it shut again to feel the release it provided. It felt really good. She slammed the cabinet shut a third time and let out a shaky breath. then poured herself a glass of wine while leaning against the counter to savor it. Suddenly, without realizing what was happening, she was crying. The anger had dissolved into hurt and sadness and simply took her by surprise.

After her kitchen cry, Sheila filled the tub and soaked. With bubbles and sea kelp scrub up to her neck, Sheila reclined in the deep clawfoot tub. She closed her eyes hoping her mind would drift for a bit to happier times. But her mind was a jumble of research thoughts, Momma Joyce, and her upcoming outing with Cy. She needed a plan of attack, but the energy wasn't there. She'd have to play it by ear in the coming days.

Sheila felt around for the tub stop with her toe to drain the water. She wrapped up in a towel and ambled to the bedroom to pick out an outfit for dinner. She wanted to be comfortable. That was one thing she knew for sure she could control for the next few hours.

Sheila took a car service to her brother's house. Another glass of wine was already calling her name. As soon as she got out of the vehicle and took a step toward the front walk, Kelly burst out the front door and rushed down the front steps.

"Where's the fire?" Sheila, wide eyed and a bit startled, stopped short.

"I tried to call you a couple of times." Kelly was out of breath and looking over her shoulder towards the house. "Your parents are here. I told Bryce not to just spring them on you, but he wanted them here for dinner too."

"Oh, crap." Sheila pulled out her phone, attempting to call the car back before her parents got wind of her presence. "I can't deal with mommy's comments tonight. I'm gonna go."

"No, Sheila. Please." Kelly intertwined her arm with Sheila's and guided her toward the front door. "I'll buffer for you if you keep your mother off my birthing hips."

Sheila laughed and rolled her eyes at the same time. "Bryce owes us a spa day!"

"Come on, Sis. I've got wine chilling just for us."

Sheila let Kelly pull her along. "Hey, guess who has a date Friday?"

"With who?" Kelly practically squealed as they entered the foyer. She clapped her hands while grinning and waiting for Sheila to put her jacket on the coat rack.

"I ran into Cy, the club owner, downtown and...shh, shh, shh." Sheila signaled they'd talk about it later once she saw her mom at the edge of the foyer. She didn't want to discuss her dating life in front of her. The divorce had given her mother entirely too much conversation fodder already. Her mom had never been keen on Kharla from the start or the idea that her daughter dated women.

"Hello, Mommy. You look nice."

"Yes, I do, Sheila. You are looking healthy as well."

Sheila stifled her desire to sigh and roll her eyes. *Healthy* was her mother's creative way of saying *fat*. She'd heard this all her life growing up. In fact, most everything her mother said had a straight edge to it. Not to her precious son though. Despite being used to it, her mother's attitude toward her still hurt. Sheila quickly made her way past her and stepped further into the house. Bryce was tending to the flat top grill and singing to himself. *Enjoy yourself now, Brycee Boy!* Sheila squinted at his profile while thinking about the hell she wanted to bring down on him as if attempting to pre-curse him.

"Daddy!" As soon as Sheila saw her father sitting at the dining table, she couldn't contain her girlish glee. She was a daddy's girl through and through. Even at her age Sheila felt like a well-loved princess around him. Sheila wrapped her arms around her dad's shoulders and hugged him from behind. She leaned her head against his, then kissed his temple.

"There's my girl!" He patted her forearm and waited for her to release him, which she didn't for a good while. He just sat there, patiently, like he always did.

Sheila finally freed him from her embrace. She took a seat across from him and next to Kelly as Bryce brought out a platter of glistening, spiced chicken he'd pulled from the grill, and a bowl of glazed string beans.

"Mmm. This smells incredible, Bryce. Thanks for having me over."

"Of course. I have to have someone to test my recipes out on. Plus, I feel bad that I got the looks, *and* cooking skills."

"She hasn't missed a meal—"

"Marianne...stop." Braxton put his hand on his wife's arm.

"No, let her go, Dad. I'm sure we'll cover all the classics tonight. I wear my hair in an unflattering way, I'm a lesbian, I'm a teacher. Oh, and now I'm divorced. Right, Mommy? I'm a failure. An embarrassment. Everything I do takes away from Marianne Hudson's great accomplishments, right?" Sheila flashed a hateful glance at Bryce, then turned back to her mother. "Please...get it out before we start eating." Sheila leaned back in her seat and glared at her mother. The steam coming off her head could have powered a sauna.

"Tuh!" Marianne clucked her tongue.

"Okay, okay, okay!" Kelly waved her hands over the table. "In our house," she looked at Bryce, then back to the table, "we do not bring our squabbles to dinner. Let's enjoy this delicious food together and remember why we love one another. Please?"

The silence settled over the table until it was obvious everyone was uncomfortable.

"Well, I'm eating. Y'all can sit here all clammed up if you want to." Bryce loaded his plate with chicken and sides. "Baby, pass the potatoes, would you?"

Sheila fought the urge to fold her arms and pout when she caught her dad looking at her. He raised his eyebrows and pursed his lips as if to say, *you're better than this*. While Sheila knew he was right, she didn't want to be the bigger person for once. She was tired of being the *Strong Black Woman* amidst obvious bias.

"You know what..." Sheila pushed her chair back. "I'm not even hungry." Sheila stood up and headed back toward the front of the house.

"Sheila...Sheila, wait." Kelly shuffled after her.

As she put her arms through her jacket, she could hear her dad chastising her mom, and Bryce describing how he had marinated the chicken for hours.

"I'm sorry, Kelly. I just don't have the energy. And I don't have to be around someone who doesn't like me."

"Your mom likes you. She loves you."

"No." Sheila shook her head. "No, she doesn't and that's her deal." Sheila took a deep breath. "Kelly, set your boundaries with her now before she thinks she can do to you what she's done to me. Bryce too. Seriously."

Kelly nodded that she understood. She wrapped her arms around Sheila and pulled her in for a hug.

"Wait, wait, wait, now." Braxton shuffled into the foyer with a plate covered in foil. "Bryce said this chicken is too good to get snubbed like that. Take this home, calm ya nerves. I'm sorry 'bout ya mama. I'm still working on her, ya know."

Sheila managed a weak smile. "I love you, Daddy. I appreciate you trying to get her to understand, but she is who she is." Sheila hugged her dad and stepped outside before he could change her mind. According to her phone the car service had several vehicles in the area. She reserved the next pickup and walked toward the end of the walkway.

It took several minutes for the car to pull up and in that time, Sheila realized she felt proud of herself. She wasn't quite sure what had come over her, but it was well overdue. The last few years she had been keeping the peace, and for what? Her life as she knew it had come crumbling down around her despite doing everything according to expectations. She was changing that now even if it meant storming out of dinner and disappointing everyone.

Sheila looked out the car window thankful for a quiet driver. She was tired. Sheila leaned to the side to check the time on the car's console. It was barely seven o'clock. Sheila was no stranger to going to bed early, but she wanted to shake off all the upset of the day. As the car pulled up to her house she decided a couple episodes of *Rosa, Rosa!* and the to-go plate her dad gave her could take the edge off. The idea of winding down with something as trivial and silly as the telenovela after completely running out of dinner in a huff truly made her giggle. The notion that her mom would have so many things to say about her behavior and that she didn't actually have to hear it made her evening activities to come all the more appealing.

"Have a good night," she called out to the driver as she stepped out onto the sidewalk. She was re-energized and hurried up the walkway. As she unlocked the door, she noticed a black car slowing across the street, then pulling off almost instantly. *That was weird,* she thought. She made sure to secure the deadbolt and draw the living room curtains so no one could peer inside. She lived in a nice neighborhood, but you could never be sure.

Sheila walked through the house turning on lights on her path to the kitchen. She removed the foil from Bryce's plate and slipped it in the microwave. While the food reheated, Sheila slipped out of her jacket and grabbed her comfy sweater from the back of the door. She turned on the tv, queued up her show, and waited for the microwave to signal it was time to eat.

Chapter 4

At 5 a.m. Sheila sat up in bed. In the dark her eyes slowly adjusted, and she strained her ears. *What is that noise?* Sheila turned her head as if that would somehow clarify what she thought she was hearing. *Knocking? Is someone knocking? Who is knocking on my door at this hour?* Sheila swung her legs over the bed and slipped her feet into her fuzzy slippers. She grabbed her robe from the end of the bed and wrapped herself up before shuffling to the front of the house.

Peering through the peephole Sheila recognized the top of her mother's head. The gray hair accenting the large circular birthmark she used to call a chocolate chip gave Marianne Hudson away.

Sheila thought twice before opening the door. She didn't have the mental acuity to go any number of rounds with mommy dearest this early in the morning, but she knew if she didn't open the door, she wouldn't be able to attend any future family gatherings without hearing about this incident over and over again.

She unlocked the deadbolt, but left the chain on, opening the door just a crack. The thought that she was hallucinating took hold and gave her cause to proceed with caution.

"Sheila, it is me. May I come in?"

She was definitely hallucinating. Her mother had never politely asked to do anything. *This should be interesting,* Sheila thought, disengaging the chain and opening the door the rest of the way.

"Mommy, it is quite early. What are you doing here?"

"I came to talk."

Sheila watched her mom as she stepped inside and took a look around. She remembered how her mom had suggested she place the furniture when she was moving in and how her placement was going to be in direct opposition to what her mom suggested. It had always been like that between the two of them. Marianne had an idea about how Sheila should do something, and Sheila went in a completely different direction. Not out of spite necessarily, but because she had her own idea about how she wanted to do things, how she wanted to live, and that seemed to be what caused the rift between them early on.

"You could have called, Mom. Like when the sun was up, I mean." Sheila shuffled toward the kitchen to put the kettle on. Her mom would want something to drink if not only to comment on Sheila's hospitality.

"You do not like talking on the phone." Marianne followed Sheila to the kitchen. "I figured this way you wouldn't be able to say no." She placed her small handbag on the counter and pushed one of the stools against the wall so she could lean back.

"Nice. Morning ambush. The tactic of mothers world-wide." Sheila yawned.

"This is not an ambush. I have some things to say, and you will listen."

Typical Marianne. Sheila moved back and forth between the stove and the sink. She placed the kettle on and pulled a selection of tea down from one of the cabinets and set it on the counter for her mom along with a small tray of sweeteners and honey.

"Mom, I'm not what you want me to be. I get it. It hurts you to see me do the things I do, and I disappoint you. Or disgust you. As the overachiever I am, probably both." Sheila pulled the kettle and poured two cups of hot water for tea.

Marianne selected her tea, Peruvian mint, and dropped it in her cup to steep.

Sheila sat down at the end of the counter. She recognized the intensity and focus Marianne applied to her cup of tea as the delaying tactic it was. She would sit there, toying with the tea until Sheila was annoyed or frustrated and willing to lash out so she could claim superiority.

But Sheila wasn't falling for it. Not like she did when she was younger. She had patience and poise now. She would maintain the peace in her own home and if Marianne didn't like it, she could leave. Sheila traced the pattern of her robe on her lap with her finger silently as the minutes ticked by.

"You look tired. You have bags under your eyes."

Sheila didn't take the bait. She kept her gaze on her mother while she sipped her tea.

"Did you get some of Bryce's chicken? I saw your dad made you a plate." Marianne took a tentative sip of tea and licked her lips. "This tea is nice."

Sheila yawned into the back of her hand. *This is what she wanted to talk about at 5 a.m.? Hmph. She's losing her touch.* Another yawn fell into her palm. It had been some time since she'd had to be up at this hour and her nerves were wearing thin.

"Okay, Marianne. This little charade has gone on long enough." Sheila was surprised how even and low her voice came out. "You didn't come over here, at this hour, to talk. You came to, I don't know, intimidate? To see if your problem child could be reined in like in years past. Well..."

Sheila stood up from the counter, and ducked her head into the kitchen to make sure the stove was turned off. She flipped the light off as she passed the counter and made her way through the living room.

"It's a no for me." Sheila didn't wait for a reply. She simply made her way back to her bedroom. She could only imagine the look on her mother's face sitting there in the dark being ignored.

A few minutes later, after she'd slid back into bed Sheila heard mumbling. It grew closer and closer until she could feel her mother's presence in the doorway of her bedroom.

"Despicable! You...You are no daughter. I didn't raise you to be gay and insolent! Apologize to me right now."

Sheila made violent snoring noises while trying to stifle her laughter. She added a twitch and a leg jerk to her theatrics.

"Wait 'til your father hears how you have disrespected me!" Marianne stomped her foot and pouted. The continued antics made her leave the bedroom. The slamming front door shook the entire house.

Sheila blew out all her air. She had been holding her breath the entire time. Folding down the covers, she poked her head out and listened. Nothing. Her mom had really stomped out and slammed the door.

"Brat!" Sheila burst into hysterical laughter after hearing her voice bounce off the walls. Her chest felt lighter. Sheila breathed deeply and felt the relief of knowing she had finally set down the idea of keeping the peace. She had to live for herself forever here on out and not worry about anyone else's feelings about it.

Sheila drifted in and out of dreamless sleep until the alarm finally went off at seven thirty. She stayed in bed just luxuriating. She really did feel different. The change seemed to have started before the early morning assault by her mother and was morphing into a new perspective all together. Sheila found herself emerging with a new attitude about how she wanted to move forward. The best way to embrace this new life view was to get excited about her date Friday with Cy.

Swinging her legs over the edge of the bed, Sheila got up and walked over to the closet. *What am I going to wear?* A sense of anticipation washed over her. Who would've thought she'd be going out on a first date after being married for eight years? Certainly not Sheila.

The silky sleeves of a black blouse tickled her palm, and a pair of sequined trousers made her think of the New Year's Eve party she'd gone to a couple years ago. The energy she used to put into going out and entertaining used to feel so natural. She was going to have to work at it now.

Two outfits made the final cut; a casual shirt dress she could pair with accessories and a dressy pair of slacks with a flowy top and hung them on the hook by the floor length mirror. She stood there for a few minutes in front of the mirror assessing herself. Aside from a few dark circles under her eyes, Sheila felt confident. She looked good. Her skin was smooth and glowy and the light in her eyes seemed to be returning. Early morning low-impact walks had brought back a bit of definition in her legs. The post-divorce regimen was working.

It was still cool outside when Sheila stepped out for the day's morning walk. The air was still as she stood on the wrap around porch stretching before she started her trek around the neighborhood. She completed a two-mile route at least four days a week. The routine had really helped keep her mind intact during the early stages of the separation and the added bonus was that her behind was tighter than ever now.

Sheila slipped one ear bud in and started off on her walk. The walk began towards the old tobacco factory that had recently been renovated into high-price apartments. Sheila had considered one of those units until she'd toured the place. Too many students from the college and young marketing types.

There was an old mom and pop bakery two blocks past that, but Sheila always turned left at the park to make the loop around the neighborhood. Around the gas station on 6th, she started feeling the burn in her buns, but she kept going. She was really starting to feel the cool morning air sinking in her lungs when she noticed a black car driving unusually slow on the far side of the road.

It was like the driver was looking for an address or something, slowly inching forward, stopping, then continuing. Almost keeping pace with her. Sheila pumped her arms harder and kept going to the next block before her turn. She had one more lap around the block and she could count her exercise done. Her plans for the day included getting to the library early and getting as much work done as possible then stopping by her office to check the mail.

Sheila immediately noticed the black car parked three houses down from hers when she turned the corner. The driver's side window was cracked a bit. Were they following her? Was somebody watching her? An uneasiness fell over her as she approached her home. Slowing her stride and crouching down under the pretense of tying her shoe, she pulled out her phone instead in an attempt to take down the license plate.

It must have been obvious because the car pulled off in a hurry before she could get the bulk of the plate's digits. Sheila stood back up and looked around. Was she really being watched?

It couldn't have been a coincidence that she saw that same car around the block and across the street the other night when she returned from Bryce's. She started toward her house, carefully watching for anyone out of the ordinary. Upon entry was when most people were attacked. A safety seminar she'd attended at the college had lodged that fact in her head.

The thought gave her chills. She pulled her keys from her pocket and positioned them between her knuckles before jogging up to her house. She placed her body in a side stance as she unlocked the door just in case. Once inside she did a quick sweep of the house, her heart racing. It was all clear, but the feeling of being watched was still all over her like sweat.

Instead of getting ready for the library, Sheila made other plans. She had to make sure her house was secure and that she was safe.

Chapter 5

The museum was beautifully set up for the multiple events taking place. Lanterns and colorful lights made dancing shadows against the building and ground. A red carpet led from the entrance down the steps out front with ushers directing people.

Sheila stood off to the side with the tickets for the Woman Warrior exhibit waiting for Cy. Every few minutes she checked her reflection in the glass at the ticket booth. She'd chosen to wear a simple black and white paneled leather skirt and a black three-quarter length top with a great silhouette. In honor of the exhibit, she donned a wide mirrored necklace that mimicked body armor and bangles.

Sheila flipped her straightened hair off her shoulder and from the corner of her eye she caught a glance of Cy stepping out of a black town car. Sheila's mouth dropped open. Her date was stunning in charcoal gray slacks that strained across her thighs with each step, a black turtleneck with a black criss cross harness cradling her chest. She strode up the steps as if in slow motion, turning heads with each step. Sheila took a deep breath. *What have I gotten myself into?*

The smile spreading across Cy's face as she grew closer sent the butterflies in Sheila's stomach racing. She couldn't believe at her big age she was feeling like this, but it was a refreshing feeling.

"Hello, Dr. Hudson. Sheila."

"Hey."

"You look—" They both spoke at the same time, then laughed.

"You look great. Seems like we both got the memo about black."

"It felt like the right choice. I think the warrior women would approve."

"Most definitely."

Sheila couldn't pull her eyes away from the chest harness. The circular ring in the middle drew attention to her chest and straps. Her fingers itched to touch it, but she restrained herself. Sheila held up the tickets. "Should we go in?"

"Yes, I'm excited for the Dahomey. I've read they were ruthless against their enemies." Cy mimicked sword work and battle moves toward an invisible enemy.

"Okay, I see you got skills. I don't know if they're holding auditions, though." Sheila laughed and led the way.

Inside they handed over the tickets and the usher directed them to the last corridor past the *History of Fashion* and *Miniatures From Around the World* exhibits.

There were various colored shields on the floor belonging to the different tribes leading to the entrance. The sound of drums pumped through the speakers above the doorway followed by tribal calls.

"I have chills!"

"Come on. I think we go this way." Cy led the way to the first interactive station. "There might be tryouts after all."

Sheila pressed the button to start the short video before Cy could. She needed something to distract her, aware of how she'd been ogling Cy ever since she walked up the steps outside. She didn't want to seem shallow, or creepy, but the woman was *fine*. Capital F-I-N-E. Her one dimple was working overtime each time she smiled and now that she wasn't wearing a jacket, her shoulders, even beneath the turtleneck, showed that she worked out. Sheila was going to have to take an extra pill for her blood pressure if this played out.

She snuck another glance at Cy who seemed to be engrossed in the video while bopping to the music. Muscled women in loincloths danced and undulated with sharp sticks in their hands. It was practice for battle, but it was also very sensual. The sweat dripping down bare abdomens and muscles flexing drew her eye back to the screen.

"You're studying that screen awfully hard." Cy turned her megawatt smile on Sheila.

"I'm testing you on it later."

"Okay, professor."

"Come on. I think the weapons display is next."

The two women looked at everything in the exhibit, talking and laughing the entire time, posing questions to stump each other in a type of verbal foreplay. It was one hundred percent working on Sheila. She'd forgotten how nice it was to have intelligent conversation and to be kept on her toes.

Near the end of the exhibit there was a warrior photo booth. They donned paper warrior garb and posed in elaborate fight stances.

"Oh my god you're so good at that!" Sheila said. "I think you were an Amazon in a previous life."

"Can you imagine? Fighting to the death, battling for the safety of your people." Cy clucked her tongue. "Chile, not me. I like a soft life."

They both laughed and exited with their souvenir photos and swords. The place they'd chosen for dinner was just a few blocks south of the museum. They took their time, strolling and continuing the conversation.

"So, you exclusively study women in various landscapes, right? Have you ever found any surprises?"

Sheila beamed at a chance to talk about her work. She stepped into the restaurant after Cy politely opened the door and waited for her to enter.

"Yes, and yes. It's incredible. Especially unearthing the women behind things we thought were created by men. Or the women who lived as men to be able to do the things they wanted to do. It's a history unto itself. And so many of them were queer. It blows my mind."

They sat down at a corner table with warm amber light. After the server took their beverage orders, Cy encouraged Sheila to continue. She did for a bit, but once they placed their food orders, she changed the subject.

"Hey, tell me what it's like owning a business? It seems very intricate."

"Oh, definitely. I think that's why I enjoy it. I have a lot of irons in the fire at any given time and something will go wrong no matter what. But it makes me have to trust and rely on people, so I think that's good."

"Do I hear a bit of type A personality coming out?"

Cy bit her lip and widened her eyes. "Guilty. I've gotten so much better over the years though, I promise."

"Good to hear."

They took a break in conversation when their food arrived to *ooh* and *ahh* over the plates. Whole fried grouper, fresh greens, and a fragrant lemony broth had other patrons turning towards their table.

After a few bites Sheila asked another question. "Is it hard working with all those beautiful women?"

Cy shook her head. "To be honest, no. Plus I don't really interact with the dancers. I have a floor manager, Tig, who does that. She's a former body builder and she doesn't take any crap. I'm sure a less restrained person would be distracted, but I'm in it for the money. I hate to say it that way, but it's true."

"Nothing wrong with that. I often wish what I did was more lucrative, but I get by, I guess."

"My folks were less than enthused when I opened the club. I never thought I was going to hear the end of it. Until I was able to pay off their mortgage and get my pop the riding lawnmower of his dreams." Cy chuckled and scooped a hearty bite of fish into her mouth.

"I know my dad is proud of me," Sheila started. "He tells me every chance he gets. Me and my mom, on the other hand, do not get along. She showed up at my house at 5am the other day to fight. I didn't have it in me."

"That's tough. Moms, they have certain ideas for us, don't they?"

Chewing her greens, Sheila nodded until she could swallow and resume talking. "They sure do. I've finally just had to walk away from her. Especially after everything that's happened the last couple of years. I can't be a people pleaser at this stage in my life."

"Cheers to that!" Cy tapped her glass to Sheila's and sipped. She paused and set her utensils down, keeping eye contact with Sheila. "So, a question for you."

"Sure. What do you want to know?"

"You were married before, right? Are you and your ex, you know, done? I don't want—"

"We are absolutely, one hundred percent done. I wouldn't have allowed a date if the ink on the divorce papers wasn't dry."

Sheila hated that this was even something that had to be said. But Cy had every right to question it. A lot of people separated and carried on affairs only to get back with their spouse. But Sheila was without a doubt not going back to Kharla. Not after what she'd done.

Cy nodded, then smiled. "Okay then." Cy tipped her glass to the air and took another sip. The questions went back and forth throughout the rest of the meal and they both seemed to be enjoying themselves.

"So, how about dessert?"

Sheila wrinkled her nose. She'd seen what the restaurant had on its menu, several pudding-y dishes that didn't exactly say dessert to her.

"You got something in mind? 'Cos, I don't think rice pudding with honey is gonna cut it for me." She hoped she wasn't being too picky, but she was not wasting this new self-awareness on pudding.

"There is an ice cream place a block back toward the museum. It's, mmmphf!" Cy kissed her fingertips.

Sheila grabbed the check before there could be any discussion about it. "Lead the way."

On the walk to the ice cream shop Sheila asked Cy about her mother's birthday.

"Let me tell you that little lady put away so much cake. She was absolutely high off sugar before we even got to the presents."

Sheila giggled. She pictured a short geriatric racing around the room like a kid, happy to have an audience. "That is too cute. I bet she had a blast."

"Yeah, Pop said she hardly slept the night before. She was so excited to see everyone. My Aunt Bebe flew up from Florida. They've been giggling like schoolgirls ever since."

Set up like an old school ice cream parlor with mint green walls and red swivel stools and black and white checkered floor tiles, the ice cream shop was buzzing. It was obviously a popular spot with great reviews and a huge following especially on date night.

"Oh, boy." Sheila said, absently looking at all the flavors. "I don't know what to get."

Cy stepped up to the menu board and pointed out a few of her favs. "The bing cherry goat cheese is really good."

"Goat cheese ice cream? I don't know about that." Sheila wrinkled her nose up at that suggestion. "What else?"

"Cinnamon chai has tons of flavor. The spices pop on your tongue." Cy turned to Sheila and raised her eyebrows. "And my personal favorite is the bourbon peach cobbler. That's what I'm having."

"I think I'll go with the cinnamon chai."

They ordered. The line was moving steadily, but their elbows kept bumping. Whenever the line moved Sheila stayed close. The slight contact was enough to make her feel warm. She liked this woman. A lot.

They stood outside eating their ice cream. Sheila was deep into her cinnamon chai review. "This reminds me of Moravian cookies at Christmas time. My tongue is tingling."

"Oh, yeah? Can I have a taste?"

Sheila's mouth fell open. *Can she have a taste?* She swallowed hard. Sheila licked her lips. "Sh-sure." Sheila licked her lips again and tried to stay relaxed. She watched Cy move closer. She had her spoon out and swiped just a bit of the ice cream off the top without averting her eyes from Sheila's face. She held the spoon in her mouth and closed her eyes.

"Mmm. Yeah, that's delicious."

"Ahh, yeah it is." Sheila felt like she was going to melt right where she stood. Laughter bubbled up in her throat and she could hardly control herself. This was so dangerous. "How's yours?"

"It's so rich and creamy. Subtle at first, then the sugar dusted pie crust pieces dance on my tongue before dissolving. Would you like to try a bite?" Cy already had the perfect bite ready on her spoon. She held it out to Sheila.

"Yes, please." Sheila opened her mouth and enveloped the spoon. She hoped she looked cute doing it but forgot all about that when the rich flavor of peaches and cream met her tongue. It was rich and creamy. "Okay, now that is out of this world good."

"Agreed. We'll have to come back and try all the flavors."

Sheila nodded. Her mind was elsewhere. She wanted to sample all of Cy's flavors right then and there. But the date was clearly winding down. She couldn't ask Cy to come back to her place, could she? *Too soon. Entirely too soon.* Sheila cleared her throat. "Did you drive tonight?" It was an innocent enough question. Maybe Cy could give her a ride home.

"No. I took a car service."

"Me too." *So much for getting a ride tonight,* Sheila thought.

They both fumbled for their phones to call a car.

"Next time let's share a car. Or I can come pick you up?"

"Yeah. I'd like that." Sheila's desire was restored. She would just have to wait a little bit to satisfy it.

Chapter 6

By Wednesday of the next week Sheila had managed to get an alarm system with video surveillance installed on her property. She hadn't managed to dissuade Kharla from calling and bombarding her with messages all hours of the day and night though.

It had crossed her mind that Kharla could have been the one driving by and camping out across the street in the black car, but she didn't have any proof. Then there was also Momma Joyce and John leaving messages for her to come to dinner in equal quantity as well. But it just didn't feel right to go over to their house or to see them right now.

The one person she had wanted to hear from, Cy, wasn't exactly blowing up her phone though and that made her feel some kind of way. She told herself if she hadn't heard from Cy by Thursday she'd call and follow up on that *next time* they'd casually mentioned. It occurred to her that she was being *thirsty* as the young folk said. She needed to turn her focus back to her research, but she was completely distracted by how pent up she was.

Sappho died in the middle of trying to reconnect with herself last night and of course she didn't have the right size batteries on hand to remedy the situation. There was no release to be found anywhere and it was making her cranky.

She went to the kitchen to make a sandwich thinking sustenance would fill the void. It couldn't hurt. She smacked on a couple of slices of turkey while she rummaged for mustard, olives, cheese, and other accoutrement for her snack.

Instead of a sandwich she decided to make a charcuterie board. After being bent over in the fridge trying to read expiration dates Sheila decided bread and spreads were too much work. She figured the charcuterie would be a fun little collection to pick at while she outlined a section of her paper.

Once the board was full with a wide selection she brought everything over to the coffee table and settled.

"Mmmphf!" Sheila didn't hold back. She tried to simply enjoy the sounds of her grazing as she packed pickles dipped in cream cheese into her mouth. "This is good. I should open a place. Sheila's Charcuterie. To hell with teaching."

Her phone rang while she was plotting out the menu for her new restaurant. "Sheila's Charcuterie. The pickles are extra!"

There was a hearty laugh on the other end. "Do you deliver? I'd love a small board." It was Cy. Her sultry voice snaked through the phone and practically made Sheila moan. She hurried to swallow the bite of cracker she'd just taken.

"Cy." She could hardly get her name out around a mouthful of Ritz. She cleared her throat. "Cy. Hi. Hey. I was just joking around."

"You're telling me I can't get any thinly sliced deli meats today?"

"Best I can do is a few olives." Sheila wondered if her smile carried through the phone. She was so happy to hear Cy's voice. It was like a balm over all her aches.

"Well, this doesn't bode well for your first review."

"I'm sure there is something I can do to make up for it." Sheila dropped her voice as she leaned back on the couch. "How are you?"

"I'm okay. I'm good. How are you?"

"Same. Took a break for a snack and now I'm changing careers."

That made Cy laugh. "I meant to call you sooner, but I had to be in Chicago for a few days."

"Business stuff?"

"Yeah. A vendor was holding several cases of booze hostage. It happens."

"Oh. That required a trip, did it?"

"Mmhm. I went straight to the parent company. You'd be surprised what a little face to face can do to get what you want."

Sheila swallowed hard. She wanted a face to face more than Cy could probably imagine. "I bet it doesn't hurt."

"I could show you. Saturday if you're free."

"What'd you have in mind?" Sheila didn't really care what Cy suggested. She wanted to see her.

"I was thinking you could come over to mine and I'd cook dinner for you."

"Ooh, that sounds promising. Can I bring anything?"

"How about something sweet?"

"Do you like chocolate?"

"I think you know the answer to that." Cy's voice was different suddenly, strained beneath the notes of excitement.

"Send me your address."

"Yes, ma'am."

Sheila tossed her phone on the couch beside her. She beat her feet against the coffee table and squealed. "Face to face! You got a second date, Dr. Hudson!" She felt a bit of relief from all her pent-up energy.

Sheila continued her second date celebration while she ate from her tray. Her mind tried to go back to managing her day, but she was buzzing. The article she wanted to review was going to have to wait. The words weren't sticking after two passes, and she didn't want to give it any more time. She wanted to prolong the excitement coursing through her and fantasize about the upcoming Saturday's events.

She grabbed her phone off the couch cushion hoping Kelly would be free for a little shopping and girl talk. The phone just rang until the voicemail picked up. Sheila would have to find someone else to share her good news with.

• • • •

On Saturday a light, romantic rain set the tone for Sheila's second date. Slow and calm was the vibe. But Sheila couldn't get a handle on her nerves. She had to keep walking into the kitchen to shove her face in the freezer to keep from sweating her makeup off. Knowing she needed to manage her expectations, Sheila paced back and forth from the kitchen to the living room hyping herself up. "You are a sexy, intelligent woman. This second date will be a piece of cake." The words she was saying to herself were one hundred percent true, but her imagination was doing overtime and running wild, along with her sweat glands.

"Ugh," she grumbled as she dashed into the kitchen again to cool off in front of the freezer. When she pulled her head out this time, she thought she heard the wind and rain picking up. Sure enough, when she looked out the kitchen window the rain had gone from a drizzle to a more driving rain. Crossing over to the living room she turned on the television to the weather channel for an update. Rain was her least favorite to drive in. If it was going to get any worse, she would take a car service instead of driving her own. *Although,* she thought, *if the date doesn't go well, I don't want to have to awkwardly wait for a ride.*

She shut the tv off before the meteorologist for her area came back on and darted into the bathroom to take the rollers out of her hair. In the mirror she fancied that she looked like a pin-up from the 40s, light makeup, deep, dark red lips. She smoothed her hands over the lace camisole, a sort of final check before she slipped into her wrap dress. The forest green dress was a favorite of hers, comfortable and flowy with a bit of rouching at the hip. It was also easy to get into...and out of. *Just in case.*

Sheila tied her dress at the hip and ran her fingers through her hair one last time before grabbing her phone and purse to leave. Halfway out the door she remembered she was bringing dessert and scurried back inside. She trotted over to the kitchen and pulled a three-layer chocolate ganache cake her brother made at her request out of the fridge.

After the stunt he pulled at dinner the other week, it was the least he could do to make up for it.

A final mental check and she was out the door. Once the cake was secure in the passenger seat, Sheila pulled up Cy's address on the built-in GPS in her car. A weather alert popped up as she turned onto the highway. There were multiple storm systems moving in.

If Sheila was sure about anything it was that she'd sleep well tonight. Something about a good storm and a light breeze put her to sleep like a baby.

Chapter 7

"Did you have any trouble finding the place?" Cy stood halfway in the door, pushing up her sleeves.

"No, not at all. It's a straight shot from the highway."

"Is this desert," Cy asked, reaching for the container and welcoming Sheila inside with a side hug.

"It is. Three-layer chocolate ganache cake."

"Mmm. I can't wait for all this chocolate."

I sure hope she is talking about me. Sheila slipped out of her coat and hung it behind the door. She listened to Cy go over the night's menu as she took in the space.

It was huge. Vaulted ceilings and exposed brick gave it an industrial feel, but the decor was a mix of soft whimsy and masculinity. Rich green, gold, and black textiles throughout alongside strong fixtures balanced the space. The kitchen took up the majority of the back wall, but opened into the living room so they could talk over an island bar.

"Cy, your home is beautiful! I love this exposed brick." Sheila set up at the bar and watched Cy move about her space. She was so fluid and calm in the kitchen. The complete opposite of Sheila who could burn boiling water if she tried hard enough.

"I try to keep it presentable and cozy. I was rushing around today making sure I hadn't left out anything too embarrassing." Cy chuckled as she brought a large bowl of salad out to the dining table. She was all smiles. Her shoulders were relaxed.

On the way back to the kitchen she sidled up next to Sheila at the bar and placed a light hand on her back. "You look incredible tonight."

Sheila tilted her head back just enough to gaze into Cy's eyes. "Thank you." After a long, slow, up and down appraisal, Sheila smiled and returned the compliment. "So do you." She pressed her back against Cy's hand and let the motion, along with the bar stool, swivel her into the crook of Cy's arm. The light, woodsy scent Cy wore captured Sheila's attention, and she let out a contented sound and held herself still.

It felt like a moment, but Sheila wasn't sure. Another few seconds and just like that it was gone.

"The lamb is resting. I need to fluff the couscous. Will you pick out something for us to drink?" She pointed to the wine rack behind Sheila.

"Sure. Let's see what you have." If Sheila hadn't been disappointed over the lost moment, she would have been very impressed by the wine selection. She looked for a shiraz, something fruity and rich that she knew would go with the lamb.

"I have sparkling water, too, if you don't feel like wine." Cy was back in the kitchen, zipping around.

"I think I found exactly what will go with dinner." She held up the bottle with satisfaction, then carried it to the table where an electric bottle opener awaited her.

She brought the foil and the cork to the kitchen. "How's this?" She held the cork out for Cy to sniff.

Cy playfully made a muppet of her oven mitt and pretended it could smell the cork. "Notes of cherry," she started, making Sheila laugh. Then she gently grabbed Sheila's wrist and pulled her further into the kitchen to smell the cork for real.

"It's perfect," she said. "Just like that opportunity I let pass before." She swallowed and briefly shook her head. "I should have kissed you, shouldn't I?"

They were standing close, almost touching. Sheila stepped into Cy's space. She let out a shuttered sigh. "It's not too late." She draped her arm over Cy's shoulder, letting it curl to the back of her neck and stroked her skin. She leaned in, Cy tilted her head and curved to meet her lips. Pressed up against the wall, they clung to each other, sampling, tasting, then melting. The room tilted beneath them.

Finally, needing air, they reluctantly pulled apart, both grinning and panting, and stealing short kisses and nips to sustain them.

"Thank you," Sheila said, still out of breath.

"You're...You're most welcome." Cy nodded. "Let's eat."

The spread was more than two people could finish in one sitting. Pistachio crusted rack of lamb with a spicy glaze, mint pomegranate couscous, braised yellow beets, and a fresh arugula salad.

"This is breathtaking." Sheila admired Cy's efforts while she poured their wine. "How'd you learn to do all this?"

"I learned the basics from family dinners. Pop loves to grill and barbecue. I like to help. I grab an idea or two from those food shows from time to time."

"Well, I am very impressed. I can do a few things, but if I'm being honest...I don't enjoy cooking."

"That's okay. As long as you're with me, you won't have to lift a finger in the kitchen."

"Cheers to that!"

The clink of their glasses sounded just as a clap of thunder struck. The unexpected boom made Sheila jump, spilling her wine.

"Oh, no. I'm sorry. I've been so clumsy lately."

"It's okay. Let me grab some napkins." Cy shot up and darted into the kitchen. At the same time another loud noise caught their attention.

"I think someone's at the door, Cy. Do you want me to get it?"

"Please, if you don't mind," she called out as she headed down the hall. "I need to grab napkins from the linen closet. It'll just take a sec."

Sheila checked to see if someone was at the door. It was two someone's according to the peephole. Two older looking women holding large paper grocery bags. They were giving major Cagney & Lacey vibes in their trench coats, but black and petite.

"It's two women, Cy." Sheila opened the door more curious than concerned. "Hello, can I help you?"

"Hi, Dear! Oh, you're not my Cynthia. Hi." The shorter of the two women made her way inside. She was dripping wet from the rain, but somehow looked as though she could defeat a twister. Her stance was strong, sturdy. She immediately placed her paper bag down on the entry table and slipped out of her coat. Her gray ringlets clung to her head. "Bebe, come inside, you're letting the heat out. Get out of that wet coat."

Cy returned with fresh napkins from the linen closet. "Who was at the...Mom? Aunt Bebe?" Cy looked both confused and happy to see them at the same time. "What are you two doing out in this rain? You're soaking wet." Cy rushed to help Aunt Bebe out of her wet coat. "Sheila, meet my mom, Lydia, and my aunt Bebe."

"Nice to meet you, Lydia, Bebe."

The women all exchanged handshakes and brief pleasantries.

"We brought you rations to ride out the storm. It's getting bad out there, Kiddo." Bebe handed off her bag of groceries to Cy then pointed past the living room. "Ladies room?"

"All the way down on the right. Bring Mom a towel when you come back."

Lydia headed to the kitchen with the groceries and Cy started to follow but turned back to Sheila and mouthed *I'm so sorry*.

"What is all this? Looks like you cooked for an army. Smells good."

"Mom, I'm on a date."

Sheila had re-situated herself at the table. She felt wildly out of place, like she was the one interrupting, but watching Cy, *Cynthia*, interact with her mom was adorable. She instantly went from a smooth, sensual to an excited kid in her mom's presence.

"How's the date going, Sheila?" Lydia had started unpacking the groceries into the pantry.

"We got the first kiss out of the way. That was nice."

Sheila and Lydia shared a laugh while Cy shot a slightly embarrassed look between the women.

"It's really coming down, Liddy. We should get going." Bebe handed her sister the towel she'd brought back from the bathroom.

"Cynthia's on a date, Bebe."

"You two are incorrigible." Cy wrapped her arms around her mom's shoulder and squeezed. She placed a kiss on the top of her head.

"Now, Sheila, Cynthia is my biggest joy. She is bright and kind and a little bit sensitive. However many dates you two go on, please just treat my baby right. Respect each other."

"Yes, ma'am. I will." The lump in her throat surprised Sheila. Her own mom would never be so affectionate with her, yet alone stand up for her like that. Sheila took a sip of wine to wash away the tightness in her throat.

SHEILA ON THE MEND

A loud clatter of thunder sounded, followed by a flash of lightning. Then the power flickered briefly.

"Uh-oh." Lydia looked up at her daughter. "You got candles, Bug?"

"Of course, Mom."

"Okay. Let me run to the washroom, then we'll get out of your hair."

The sound of wind and rain beating against the building grew louder. Bebe moved to stand by the window just as another flash of lightning struck.

"I think lightning just hit that tree!"

Sheila jumped up just in time to see the branches of a poplar tree cracking and falling towards the building into the road. "Whoa! That was too close for—"

Before she could finish her sentence, the power went out and stayed out this time.

"Alright, before we start bumping into things and getting hurt, everyone stay where you are. I'm bringing the lights to you." Cy was already lighting candles. "Ma," she called out.

"I'm okay. I found a flashlight under the sink."

Sheila had hooked her arm with Bebe's and guided her to the dinner table where Cy was extending one of the table leaves and arranging some votives.

"Alright, looks like this twosome is becoming a foursome."

"Might as well eat while it's still warm."

"Oh, no, Honey. We wouldn't want to intrude."

Cy scoffed loudly. "Well, you're certainly not going back out into the storm. Stop lights are probably out anyway. Sit. Eat. Tell embarrassing stories about me as you are wont to do." Cy looked over her wine glass at Sheila and raised her eyebrows.

"Lydia, come sit beside me," Sheila said, grinning. "Tell me everything I need to know about this one."

They passed plates around, critiqued Cy's cooking, and shared stories in the candlelight. Sheila had never laughed so much in her life. She had fat, glossy tears in her eyes and her stomach ached from laughing.

When she looked across the table at Cy she was in a similar state. Joy spread across her cheeks like wildfire. She caught Sheila looking at her and winked.

"Who has room for dessert?" Cy was up and clearing the table before anyone could decline.

"I can't believe the power isn't back on." Lydia followed Cy to the kitchen. "Don't you have a generator, Hon?"

"I used to, Ma. I got rid of it. Hindsight is twenty-twenty I suppose."

"I'll tell your dad to put one on your birthday list."

"You don't have to do that. I'd hardly use it."

"Better safe than sorry, Bug."

"You're right. You're right." Cy deferred to her mother's judgment.

Sheila joined them in the kitchen. "Cy, Aunt Bebe says she's not feeling too well. She wants to lie down if that's okay." She looked over her shoulder at Bebe who was massaging both sides of her head at the table.

"Of Course. Aunt Bebe, I'll set you up in the spare. Is it one of your headaches?"

"It's all that wine she drank," Lydia chimed in. "I'll come sit with you in a sec, Beebs." Lydia turned her attention back to putting dishes in the dishwasher.

SHEILA ON THE MEND

"Lydia, let me do that. I'll bring you a slice of cake when I'm done." Sheila reached for the plate and fork she held.

"A big piece?" Lydia furled her eyebrows and looked over the top of her glasses.

Sheila mimed how big a piece she would slice for her, hands wide on either side of her head.

Lydia nodded and scampered off like a kid getting away with a secret.

Sheila could hear Cy, Lydia, and Aunt Bebe teasing each other as she rinsed the last remaining plates and stacked them in the dishwasher.

She closed her eyes and took several deep breaths to ground herself. It had been an incredible night. Unexpected in many ways, but incredible nonetheless.

Cy returned to the kitchen with a smirk on her face. "Those two are old lady tipsy."

Sheila turned from the sink, nodding her head and grinning while drying her hands on a tea towel.

"I thought they might be." Suddenly Sheila didn't know what to do with her hands. She and Cy were standing a few feet apart in the kitchen. "I feel—" She wiggled her fingers up and down in front of her body like electricity had control of her.

"Oh, that appears to be very serious." Cy took a couple steps toward Sheila and opened her arms. "But you're in luck. I know a very effective treatment."

Sheila stepped forward and let herself fall into Cy's arms, letting out a deep sigh.

"This has been one of the best dates I've ever had. Your mom and aunt are hilarious."

"They like you too. They're already talking about having you over for coffee and cookies before Aunt Bebe leaves to go back to Florida." Cy squeezed Sheila and placed a quick kiss on the side of her head.

They stood there just holding each other for a while listening to the rain and each other's uneven breaths.

"So, Cynthia—"

Cy shook her head. "Now you know my secret. My kryptonite."

"Oh, yeah? That'll get me whatever I want, huh? Call you what your mother calls you?"

"She told you I'm sensitive."

"I won't abuse it, how 'bout that?" Sheila let her hands roam over Cy's back, kneading her muscles.

"I think you're trying to get me in trouble." Her sing-song tone indicated it was working.

"I think you're trouble," Sheila whispered, planting a light kiss on Cy's throat where her pulse thumped wildly.

"Are you comfortable staying over? It's not really letting up and I think several trees are down. I would hate to worry—"

"You're very kind, you know that?" Sheila let her hands rest against Cy's chest. Part of her wish for the evening was coming true, but it would be an undoubtedly chaste night with Lydia and Bebe just down the hall.

There was also the matter of nerves. They were both too hesitant for anything to happen tonight and it was probably for the best. The amount of wine imbibed tonight took away any notions of consent already.

"After I find you pajamas and pillows would you want to sit and talk? We still haven't had dessert."

"I'm actually starting to feel the effects of all the wine we enjoyed tonight. I'm part of the old lady brigade too, I guess."

Sheila woke up in the middle of the night. Her head felt twice as big as normal, and the sound of rain seemed to be coming from somewhere behind her eyes. After a few minutes sitting in the dark, she remembered she was in Cy's bed. Alone.

The sheets were silky against her skin as she slid her legs over the edge of the bed. She hoped she would be able to find her way to her purse in the dark.

Shuffling toward where she thought the door was, Sheila made her way back to the living room. Muted blue light glowed from the tv. Cy was stretched out on the couch with one arm tucked under her head looking absolutely relaxed in partial slumber.

"When did the power come back?"

Cy shifted and stretched beneath her blanket. "About an hour ago. You couldn't sleep?"

"Headache. I need my blood pressure meds." Sheila moved toward the bar where she'd left her purse aware of how she must look in the oversized Steelers shirt and jogging shorts Cy had provided. "Are you watching *Rosa, Rosa!?*"

"Busted. I was just catching up on a few episodes."

"I love this show. I got hooked in college. My roommate got me into it."

"Really? I thought I was single-handedly keeping them on the air."

"Yes! I usually save up a week's worth and binge while grading papers." Sheila turned her attention to the screen and leaned her hip on the arm of the couch.

"Hey," Cy flipped the edge of her blanket open in invitation. "You sure?"

"*Rosa, Rosa! Los gemelos desde el nacimiento ahora son enemigos de por vida!*"

Sheila clapped her hand over her mouth to mute her giggles. The theme song was the most ridiculous part and Cy's singing was so bad. She snuggled in next to Cy who promptly tucked the blanket over her lap and wrapped an arm around her.

Chapter 8

"You've been doing this every...day?" Darcy was out of breath. She unzipped her jacket and shrugged out of it.

Sheila chuckled and pumped her arms harder. "It's great. At first, I thought exercising would help me get my sexy back, but it's so much more. I feel more clear headed, I'm sleeping better, I have more energy."

"I bet your stripper friend is loving that." They turned the corner on the college track for the second time.

"She owns the club, she's not a stripper. And they're called exotic dancers."

Darcy stretched out her arm, brushing Sheila's shoulder, signaling that she needed to take a break. Darcy bent over at the waist and put her hands on her knees. "Well, I'm sure your ladylove appreciates the extra energy in the sack."

Sheila stretched her right arm over her chest, then the left while stepping in place. After the stormy sleepover she and Cy had gone to the symphony, a concert in the park, a drag bingo fundraiser, a Steelers game, and a handful of dinners. They were becoming intimate on a number of levels except a sexual one and as far as she could tell the tension was building. Another reason Sheila kept up with the daily walking.

"We haven't actually had sex yet."

"Uh-oh. What's wrong with her?"

Sheila tried to hide her reaction, but her brows raised and pulled her eyes wide. "There's nothing wrong with her. Or me for that matter. We're dating and we're having fun."

Darcy mushroomed her lips out and bugged her eyes in question. "Well, Edwin and I must be *dating* and *having fun* too. His momma is camped out in my sunroom for the next two weeks. She popped up unannounced. She leaves her teeth laying around on my kitchen counters, the couch. I almost sat on them yesterday. Her chompers definitely don't help get me in the mood."

"Oh, that's gross!"

They posted up in front of a set of bleachers to stretch and keep talking in the sun. The lacrosse team ran early morning drills back and forth across the field.

"We should get together. Do a double date. I want to meet your gal."

Sheila perked up at the idea. She wouldn't mind showing off Cy for a night. "I'll see when Cy is free. We'll set something up." The smile on her face spread wide.

"Has she met your family yet?" Darcy bent down to tie her shoe and groaned.

"No, not yet. My dad has been avoiding me since my blow up with Marianne. I'm actually going over to the house after this to return a screwdriver I've had for the last six years."

"He's going to see right through that," Darcy laughed while doing her side bends.

"I know, but I miss my daddy." The thought of a rift between them was making her stomach hurt. "You got time to get smoothies before class?"

"You're buying. I gotta save my money for muscle cream after this torture walk."

Sheila stopped at Soul Sandwich Cafe to pick up coffee and sandwiches for her and her dad. What few conversations they'd had since the 5am Marianne debacle had been short and weird, and Sheila didn't like it.

The one person that had been the steady constant in her life seemed to have a problem with her now and it didn't feel good at all. She wasn't sure how any conversation they had today was going to go, but she at least wanted to stop by and see him. Marianne was at her swimming for seniors class this morning so Sheila figured it was a good time to swing by the house. She pulled up and parked on the street in front of her childhood home. The front door was open, letting in the morning light.

"Dad, it's Sheila. I brought breakfast." She called out from the entryway.

"In the kitchen!" The sound of Braxton's booming voice energized Sheila and moved her forward. She was reassured instantly.

As soon as Sheila entered the kitchen she stopped in her tracks. Her mouth fell open in utter dismay. Her father stood over the kitchen island with a mechanic's rag covered in grease and what smelled like gasoline. There were lawn mower parts spread out over newspaper on the counter.

"Mom's going to have a conniption if she sees this."

"That's why she's not going to see it." Braxton huffed with a smile on his face. "Hey, Punkin. You said you brought breakfast?"

Got'em! Sheila placed the sack of sandwiches on the side counter along with the coffees. The man could eat all day, every day. It was one of his favorite pastimes. Sheila knew that was her in. "I stopped at Soul Sandwich. I know you like their brisket and egg."

"Mmhm." Braxton stood at the sink scrubbing his hands and splashing water on the floor.

Sheila took her breakfast to the table. She thought about how she was going to broach the subject of her mom while unfolding the wax paper from around the bagel. The more she thought about it, the more nervous she got. Taking a bite of her bagel and egg white she instantly wished she'd gotten the brisket and egg sandwich too. Braxton stood against the counter eating his breakfast, stopping occasionally to lap up the sauce and egg yolk running out the side of the sandwich. He was three or four bites into it and almost done.

Sheila sipped her coffee. She hated how awkward this felt. There wasn't a time she could remember when she and her dad sat not talking and carrying on with each other. This wasn't right. "Hey, Dad, can we talk?"

"Of course. What's on your mind?"

Sheila got up to toss her sandwich wrapper in the trash and came to stand against the wall with her hands behind her. "Feels like we've been avoiding each other since the blowup with Mom. What's that about? Are we good?"

"Yeah, yeah. Just busy is all. I've been helping Uncle Jerry at the shop here and there. You know how it is." Braxton took the lid off of his coffee and took a big gulp. He turned his attention back to the greasy mower parts, fiddling with screws and bolts.

"That's it, huh? Just busy?"

"Mmhm."

"You're not mad at me? I know Mom is mad at me. It wouldn't be a stretch if—"

"Not mad...just a little disappointed. You're bigger than—"

"I'm bigger than this. Yeah, you've said that my entire life." Sheila felt like she did as a kid. Having to be the bigger person when dealing with all matters from her mother. It hurt that after all these years that was the stance her father would continue to take instead of just taking her side. She was disappointed too. "Does she ever have to be the bigger person?" Sheila waited for an answer, but she didn't get one. "She showed up at my house at 5 a.m. to start a fight, Dad. If she felt disrespected, she brought it on herself." Sheila felt herself wanting to pout and shut down.

"I'm just surprised after all she's done for you, Sheila." Braxton set the clutch down abruptly causing it to roll into another part on the counter.

Sheila felt blindsided. *All she's done for me?* Sheila shifted onto her right leg, unable to control her face. Her shock and confusion wore like a kabuki mask tight on her skin.

"She's accepted you at every turn and loved you despite your choices."

"Love looks a helluva lot different over here where I'm standing. You can't expect me to feel respectful and appreciative of someone whose bare minimum acceptance, *despite my choices*, as you say, causes me pain on a daily basis."

Sheila felt her chest tightening against her every breath. She didn't come over to fight with him. But this news, that he thought her mother was in some way entitled to more respect, yet alone any, after her continued rancor towards her, was beyond her.

"Despite my choices," she muttered to herself over and over. Her mind whirled. She'd folded her arms over her chest, not in defense, but to comfort herself. This sounded like someone she didn't even know, and it hurt. "You don't think I make good choices? What..."

"Divorce, Sheila? We didn't raise you to—"

"Stand up for myself? To demand the respect I deserve?" Sheila couldn't help raising her voice. She felt her world spinning out of control. The tears plopped out of her eyes before she could stop them. "Kharla cheated on me! She was lying at every turn. I should have stayed for that?"

"I did!" Braxton slammed the mechanic's rag down and hung his head.

The sound of the refrigerator humming filled Sheila's head with noise. She tilted her head as if to clear it, but what her father had just admitted clouded everything. Blinking didn't help either. "Wha...*You* did? What does that mean?" Sheila felt the egg whites trying to come back up. "What does that mean?" She spoke more stern this time, tears welling up in her eyes again. "Dad..." This time her voice was softer. She just wanted confirmation. An answer, some bit of knowledge that would clear everything up.

A strangled sob, like the sound of an animal's last breath escaped Braxton's mouth as he turned to Sheila. His eyes darted around the room before closing. "I never wanted you to find out. I knew it would make you hate her even more, but then you and Kharla...And it brought everything back to the surface."

"Mom cheated on you..." Sheila had never seen her Braxton look so old. She noticed all the wrinkles carved into his forehead and the sunspots on his hands and arms. His vibrant ruddy color was pale. He looked every one of his seventy-six years in front of her now. "Why did you—"

"I love your mom despite—"

"Her choices." Sheila felt herself trembling all over. That he truly knew the hurt and betrayal of someone he trusted and loved made her back teeth ache. The thought that her divorce reminded him of that betrayal whenever he looked at her hurt even more.

Then, like an arrow to the chest, the thought that she herself reminded him of that betrayal shook her to the core. "Oh, my god!

Oh, my god! Am I...?" She stopped before verbalizing what she already suspected to be true.

The silence was enough to shatter her world. Sheila swallowed hard. The egg white bagel was making a return trip. She turned and ran down the hall to the bathroom off the den. The bathroom door bounced off the wall, sending the doorstop into a frenzy of funny cartoonish noises. Sheila clung to the toilet until her stomach, still contracting, was empty. After a few deep breaths Sheila was back to standing. She snatched the hand towel off the holder and wet one end in the sink. Like her father used to do when she was a child, she placed it on the back of her neck.

A light knock on the doorframe made her look over her shoulder. Braxton had come to check on her. She waved him off. "Just...gimme a minute, please."

He was sitting at the table when she came back out to the kitchen with his elbows on his knees and his head down. Braxton looked up, his face pinched. "You'll always be my daughter, Sheila."

Sheila tried to blink away a new cache of tears before they crested, but it was too late. She nodded her head acknowledging her father's words. "I'll talk to you later, okay." She hugged him quickly, then left before he could say anything else.

The drive home was a blur. It's a wonder she made it home without incident. As soon as she got inside, she went to the bathroom to strip down. The smell of vomit lingered on her somewhere and she had a headache from crying. She brushed her teeth and took a shower. Then immediately climbed into bed. The cold sheets made her shudder, but she wanted to go numb. She just wanted to sleep and wake up to none of what she now knew. But there was no shutting down her thoughts.

There was no way to go back to before. Her mother's lifelong mistreatment started to make sense. An affair child that threatened to upend everything by just existing would be hard to ignore, hard to love. Sheila realized just how much her dad's overcompensating for Marianne's behavior had kept the balance all these years. He likely resented her and tried to push her to be the bigger person because he already knew how his wife would behave. *You're bigger than this,* he'd always say. Now Sheila wondered if he'd been saying it for her benefit or his own. Sheila closed her eyes just hoping for some kind of clarity she could grab on to, but once the floodgates on her tears broke free, she couldn't stop crying.

She had just dozed off when the doorbell alerted her to someone standing out front on her porch. Not wanting to be bothered was an understatement. She wasn't in the mood for anything. Not an insurance salesman, a girl scout, nothing.

When she snatched the door open, ready to give whoever it was a piece of her mind, she only saw Momma Joyce standing there with a potted plant and she burst into tears again.

Momma Joyce ushered her back inside and shut the door behind her, cooing and assuring her that she was alright. She set the plant down on the coffee table and steered Sheila to the couch. Her short, round body gave off a warmth so welcoming Sheila clung to her.

Of all the people to show up at her house today Momma Joyce was absolutely the right one to do so. She had been nothing but loving to Sheila when she and Kharla had gotten together and even now seemed to be willing to continue providing that motherly kindness.

Sheila could hear herself blubbering incoherently, but she couldn't stop or make herself clear. When she finally took a breath, she found Momma Joyce handing her tissues from her purse and patting her leg.

"I'm so sorry I haven't called or stopped by. I thought it would be too hard to see you and John and I really don't want to see Kharla. I'm sorry if that's mean or hurts your feelings. I just can't." Sheila felt the tears rising again, but it felt good to finally say these things to her former mother-in-law.

Momma Joyce just smiled and continued to comfort Sheila. "It's okay. Kharlatta, well, she has certainly made her bed…We know she really messed up and we don't blame you. I feel partly responsible for all the hurt she caused you. Both me and John do."

"It's like it never ends, Joyce. There's always something threatening my happiness and it's too much. My mom has been especially horrendous lately and I've had enough. I fought with Dad today. Found out life altering news and now look at me, I'm snotting all over your shoulder."

"Oh, that's nothing." She looked at her blouse. "That'll come right out with detergent."

Sheila smiled. Joyce's ability to make her feel better was unmatched, and fully welcome. She turned her attention to the potted plant Momma Joyce brought with her to change the subject. "Is this from your garden?"

"It's called Aster. It'll do well in full light." She stroked the soft petals, making the stem sway.

"I love it." They sat together quietly for a bit. Sheila liked how Momma Joyce didn't need to badger her with questions or fill the room with talking. It was a quality she wished Kharla had inherited.

"I won't overstay my welcome. I know I didn't call first. I just wanted to put my eyes on you. We do miss you for what it's worth."

Momma Joyce was already up and smoothing out her lavender skirt.

"I appreciate it. Tell John hi for me. I don't know when I'll feel comfortable enough to stop by, but I'll think about it." Sheila stood up and followed her to the front door. "How did you know where I'd moved to, if you don't mind me asking?" It dawned on Sheila that she hadn't told too many people about her new house. Especially no one that ran in the same circles as Kharla and her family.

"Braxton gave us your address. I begged him. Don't be cross with him. He was telling us how you've been doing the last time we had dinner together."

"You and John still see my folks?" The idea of the four of them hanging out together didn't sit right with her, but they'd become family too after all. Sheila let it slide.

"Just every once in a while." Momma Joyce smiled. She reached up and hugged Sheila.

"I'm glad you stopped by, Joyce. I really appreciate it."

"Anytime dear."

Sheila opened the door for Momma Joyce and stepped out onto the porch with her. Up the walk she saw a tall, well-dressed club owner approaching. Cy.

"Hey."

"Hi. Bye, Joyce." Sheila waved weakly then turned her attention back to Cy.

"I called you a couple times. I thought we were having lunch today."

"I'm sorry. I forgot. I went to patch things up with my dad this morning and found out..." Sheila shook her head. The tightness in her throat restricted her breathing. She was trying to hold off yet another round of tears and broke eye contact with Cy. "I found out he's not actually my father by accident."

"Sheila, I'm so sorry. Are you...Obviously you're not okay. What can I do?" She gripped both of Sheila's arms and gave her a comforting squeeze.

"Come in. Sit with me."

"Of course."

Sheila looked over her shoulder as she moved to step inside. There, across the street, again was the black car, just idling. "Has that car been across the street this whole time?" Sheila pivoted toward the steps. She was tired of this. Whoever was watching her was about to get an up close and personal introduction.

If they wanted to watch her so badly, they would quickly learn that she didn't take this lightly. She was off the porch and down the steps before Cy knew what was happening.

What she was going to say when she got to the car hopefully would come to her. Right now she was on the attack. But as soon as she was more than halfway down the walkway the car sped off down the street, kicking up dust and squealing tires out of sight. *Yeah, you had better run!* Sheila stood on the sidewalk staring in the direction of the stalker with her hands clenched in fists down at her side, her chest heaving.

"What was that all about?" Cy caught up to her and joined her on the sidewalk.

"That black car has been watching my house, following me on my neighborhood walks. That's why I got the security system installed. I'm fed up with this!" Sheila was past her limit. Even to her own ears she sounded exhausted, deflated, and a little unstable.

"Let's go inside. We'll get to the bottom of it, okay." Cy was there with her arm around her waist, guiding her back up the walk and inside.

The fact that Cy was inside her home, looking worried about her, made Sheila a bit more aware of herself. She hadn't fully acknowledged the situation before, but now that she was standing in the middle of the living room with her hands on her hips, out of sorts, she needed to ground herself.

"Hi," she said, letting out a breath. "I'm truly sorry about lunch. I forgot." She'd said that while they were outside, but this time she was apologizing, not explaining. She let Cy fully pull her into a hug and held on.

"Just breathe, okay. Just breathe."

Sheila focused on her breath, but her mind was all over the place. She turned her attention to the light flutter of Cy's breath as it passed over her ear with each exhale. They kept breathing together until she felt a little calmer.

"Is that better?"

Sheila nodded. "A little bit, yeah." She rubbed her stomach when Cy stepped back to take a look at her. "I'm hungry. I need to eat something. I got sick this morning and then..." She looked towards the bathroom and shook her head. "There's throw up on my top in the bathroom and—"

"Sheila, let me take care of it." Cy gently led her to the couch by her hands and sat down with her. "You've had a day. Let me take care of it, let me help."

"I can do it, I can..." *Let her take care of you.* The voice in her head was loud and unrelenting. Sheila closed her eyes tight and nodded. "Okay." She watched Cy buzz around her house, looking just as at home as she was in her own space.

SHEILA ON THE MEND

"You weren't kidding about not cooking, huh? There's not much in here *to* cook." Cy's tone was light and clearly unconcerned. She was leaning against the dishwasher with her phone against her ear talking low and stealing glances over at Sheila every so often.

She brought her a cup of chamomile tea. "Food is on the way. The soiled workout top has been stain treated and vanquished to the wash. I gagged a little, but it's done. Can I look at your security cameras?"

"The thingy is on the desk." Sheila pointed to the corner where her laptop sat charging on the small desk she had set up in the corner. She sipped at the tea and watched Cy downloading and clicking away on her computer. She was on her phone again. Her voice was serious and sharp.

"Sonnie, Cy. I need a favor. Yeah. I'm sending you a couple surveillance videos. Uh-huh. Late model four door black sedan. Partial plate." Cy nodded and grinned as if the person on the other end of the call was saying something agreeable. "That's why I called. Thanks, brother."

"Are you part of the CIA or something? What was that about?"

"I want to try to get you some answers, some piece of mind. Otherwise, you gotta move in with me so I know you're safe."

"Too soon, too soon." Sheila appreciated the gesture, but she wasn't moving anywhere. "I'm sure you have some quirks and habits I'm not yet aware of. I want to figure them out first before I start packing again."

"Fair enough." Cy held her hands up in surrender and rejoined Sheila on the couch.

"Would you like to meet a friend of mine and her husband? We could do dinner sometime?"

"I'd love that. My turn to get the dirt on you."

"I never asked you how your day was." Sheila was trying to keep her mind from straying. She didn't want to start crying again.

"Calm in comparison." Cy stilled Sheila with a brief concerned look then continued on. "I think I have a thief behind the bar. We keep coming up short. Benefit of the doubt is wearing thin."

"That can't end well."

"No, it can't. It'll get resolved." Cy looked at her phone then stood up and walked over to the door. "Food." She was out the door and back in a matter of minutes. She carried what looked like ten or so grocery bags in her arms and placed them on the bar top when she reached the kitchen.

"What did you do?" Sheila was looking with vivid curiosity and started to get up.

"You stay right there on that couch." Cy rummaged through a few bags, then brought over a couple of take-out containers of food and placed them on the coffee table in front of Sheila. She returned to the kitchen and unpacked what looked like groceries—eggs, bacon, an assortment of cheeses and pre-sliced fruit, a plastic clamshell of arugula, and other things. She opened the freezer a couple of times too.

"Is that ice cream?" Sheila craned her neck to see. "From that ice cream shop?"

Cy grinned and nodded. "For later if you feel up to it."

"I feel up to it right now," Sheila said, opening the first take out container. "Oooh! Dumplings." Her attention redirected to the food in front of her.

"Who was that adorable lady that was leaving when I got here?" Cy had her own take-out container in hand.

"Thatwasmymotherinlaw." Sheila couldn't get a clear word out around the dumpling she had plopped into her mouth.

"One more time for my untrained ear."

"Sorry. I said that was my mother-in-law. Former mother-in-law. Joyce. Apparently, my folks and my former in-laws hang out still. I mean they can do whatever they want, right? They're adults. It just seems kinda weird the more I think about it."

"You feeling a little bit betrayed, maybe?"

Sheila shrugged, not wanting to delve into her feelings anymore today, although it did feel like betrayal. She investigated the other unopened take-out container on the table. It was chicken satay with peanut dipping sauce. *How did she know?* Sheila looked over at Cy who was attentively attacking what looked like pad Thai with shrimp. She was easily the sexiest thing in the room. Her jaw moved like a piston, making the chord of muscle in her neck relax and tighten over and over again.

"I needed this. Thank you." She'd said it about a dozen times since Cy had gotten to her house, but it needed to be said again. Cy was effortlessly making her a priority and it made her feel safe. It made her feel...loved.

"You're welcome." Cy finished chewing a bite then set her food on the coffee table and leaned back against the couch cushions. She reached her hand out across the couch with her palm facing up in an offer of connection and comfort.

The evening came and went. Sheila and Cy relaxed together stretched out on the couch watching tv. Sheila drifted in and out of sleep nestled against Cy's body. She felt the soft, rhythmic caress of her hands moving up and down her back, lulling her deeper into slumber.

Chapter 9

The three garters Kelly picked out looked exactly the same to Sheila. She was absolutely no help in this decision. The last few weeks she'd felt pretty useless after finding out the truth about her father.

Every time she crossed paths with an elderly Black man, she couldn't help but let her imagination spiral into thinking he could be her biological father. It was ridiculous, but she couldn't stop it from taking over her thoughts.

Even more ridiculous was how she was avoiding her father. He'd called a few days after their blowup and she'd tried to keep it together, but she kept replaying it in her mind while he asked about the insulation on her pipes. She didn't know if Braxton had informed her mother that she now knew the truth or if they were even talking to each other and he wanted to know if the pipes were wrapped.

"Earth to Sheila. You're not even listening, are you?" Kelly pouted, but she quickly moved on to a booth boasting buy one get one linens.

The Wedding Festival was so loud it was a wonder she could concentrate at all. Whose idea was it to have two hundred plus vendors set up outside at the fairground in mid-August? It smelled like manure and animals, and there was hay everywhere. A fresh hell if Sheila ever recognized one.

"I'm sorry, Kelly. My mind is a mess these days. I don't know if I'm coming or going."

"Tell me about it. We're getting so close to the wedding. I can hardly keep things straight. I understand." Kelly came around the vendor's table to stand beside Sheila. "You want to talk about it? I'm a pretty good listener."

"You are certainly that. But today is about helping you. We have to get through your list." Sheila held up the clipboard with all of the planning printouts and pictures and gave Kelly her best smile. She told herself she needed to snap out of her funk for Kelly's sake and act like she was having a good time. "I saw the cake topper people two aisles over. They have Black figurines."

"Ooh, lead the way!"

They dropped the cloth napkins and made a beeline for the cake decorations. Sheila made notes on some of the vendors they passed in case Kelly wanted to switch gears or add something later. When she saw some food carts off to the side, she darted off to grab them a couple of sandwiches.

"Good idea," Kelly said in between bites. "We have to keep our strength up."

"It's a marathon not a sprint!"

Kelly walked in a figure eight around the tables. She was looking at cake toppers, candy pearl beads, and edible flowers. "I don't think Bryce would like any of these." She scrunched up her face and went back to the first table. They at least had more of a selection. Kelly held up two little green Mr. and Mrs. alien figures and rolled her eyes.

"How are things going with you and Cy?" Kelly looked over at Sheila, her eyes eager to spot any signs of trouble.

Sheila didn't turn her attention away from some crystal hair combs that had caught her eye. "Really good actually. She's a sweetheart, funny, and kind of protective in this really subtle way. She's a great kisser. I *love* that."

"Well, that's great! I thought maybe she was the something making you distracted and in a bad mood." Kelly had come to stand beside Sheila. She looked at the hair combs and held one up to her head. The sunlight made the crystals gleam.

The last thing Sheila wanted to do was talk about what was really bothering her. Kelly was a good listener, but she'd tell Bryce the instant he was in earshot, and it was bad enough walking around with the weight of knowing everything she knew now. Sheila didn't think she had the right to blow up Bryce's life too. Or would her little brother even care?

Sheila sighed low in her chest. "My research is stalled, that's all. It's bumming me out and I can't figure out a work-around." It wasn't completely false. She was simply waiting on a few journals from the central library that were on hold.

"Your research. I see."

Sheila knew Kelly didn't believe her, but her willingness to drop it for now was greatly appreciated.

"Are you bringing Cy to the wedding?"

"Um…I haven't asked her yet, but, yeah, probably."

"Ask her already. You know she'll look good in a suit, and I bet she can dance. Can she dance?"

"Oh, yeah! She's great." Sheila plastered a big smile on her face and steered Kelly to another table with party favors. It was enough to draw her attention back to the wedding planning.

They meandered to different tables and stalls, picking out everything from center pieces for the reception to flower preservation kits for after the ceremony.

"This was such a good idea," Kelly said while loading the last few boxes of items into the back of Sheila's car. "I saved like a thousand dollars on the linens alone."

"I'm so glad. I knew you'd find a lot of things on your list. They could have set up at the coliseum though. The smell out here is wild. Literally. I'm surprised I didn't see a pile of horse shit somewhere."

Sheila secured a case of wine with a bungee cord and stuffed a towel behind the box so it wouldn't rattle on the drive to Kelly's. She got in and started the car up.

"Do you think you'll get married again, Sheila?"

"Hardball with Kelly Martin, ladies and gentlemen." Sheila tried to play it off, but she found herself gripping the steering wheel harder than necessary. Marriage was the last thing she wanted to think about for herself. "I don't know, Kelly. Probably not."

"But it wasn't all bad, right?"

"No. It wasn't." Sheila remembered a lot of good in her marriage, but the bad certainly cast a shadow over those times. The bad made her second guess herself and pick apart everything she had thought was good.

"You're not having doubts, are you?" Sheila stole a quick glance at Kelly, then turned her attention back to the road.

"No. I was just wondering." Kelly looked out the window and kept quiet for the rest of the ride home.

When Sheila pulled up to the house, Bryce was just stepping outside to help them offload Kelly's purchases into the garage. He was still wearing his chef's coat and pants and looked haggard from his latest catering gig. "What?" Bryce screwed up his face at his sister.

"What?" Sheila rolled her eyes. She had been staring at him, comparing his features to hers and Braxton's, wondering if he'd ever suspected that they had different dads. It wasn't his fault that their parents had kept the truth from them both all these years. Their mother suddenly sprang to mind. She'd probably been adamant about the truth not coming out. She might've even used it to put a wedge between her and Bryce. Marianne was always doting on her baby boy, the clear favorite. *Did he already know,* Sheila thought. She'd never been all that interested in Bryce's life, but she thought it was their seven year age difference. They didn't have too much in common to begin with. But maybe he already knew the big family secret and kept his distance on purpose. Being around Bryce now made her hyper aware of what she knew. Sheila tried to shrug it off. She walked out of the garage to grab another box from the car and clear her mind.

The last couple of boxes from the wedding festival haul fit perfectly onto the pallets Bryce had set up against the back wall in the garage. Something in the rafter caught Sheila's eye as she stood up and she jumped almost a foot when she looked up into the eyes of an inflated clown head bobbing from the garage door rack. "What the hell is that?"

Both Bryce and Kelly burst out laughing. "Some leftover Halloween thing. Bryce scares the trick-or-treaters with it."

"Dammit! It about gave me a heart attack." Sheila stormed out of the garage and slammed the hatch on her SUV. "Bryce, you're so fucking childish!" She grumbled to herself as she climbed in the driver's seat and started the car. All the anger and annoyance she was feeling wasn't all to be blamed on the clown. But she couldn't just drop everything at Bryce's feet. He wouldn't understand.

"Sheila, wait!" Kelly, ever the peacemaker, trotted over, tapping the passenger side window until Sheila rolled it down all the way. "Stay for a bit. Bryce is gonna fire up the grill. We've got chicken wings and burgers."

SHEILA ON THE MEND

"No. I need to go shower and get the stench of fairground funk out of my nose and hair. Maybe another time."

"Okay." Kelly was clearly disappointed. "Thanks for helping me with the wedding stuff today."

"You're welcome. I'll see you later, okay?"

Sheila couldn't wait to pull off. The way her shoulders felt like they were floating somewhere around her ears and her neck ached was sign number one she needed to get away from anyone who might have feelings. She wouldn't be able to hold in her irritability much longer. "Ugh!" Growling and slapping at the steering wheel only helped so much. *Everyone and their stupid happiness,* she thought. She had been happy and blissfully unaware once. Now she carried around what felt like an extra ten pounds of secrets. It wasn't fair.

The highway traffic wasn't making things any better. There was a long white church van halfway in both lanes with its hazards on. "You gotta be kidding me right now." She tried to get around the van like the car in front of her and damn near took out the driver's side headlight on the guardrail. Her phone started ringing as she nosed the SUV around the van, then back into her lane. Out of habit she pressed the answer button on the dash.

"Yeah?"

"Uh-oh. Did I catch you at a bad time?" Cy sounded as light and unaffected as ever, however disembodied through the speaker.

"I'm on the highway. I'm just in the foulest mood and everything is pissing me off."

"Not everything I hope."

"You know what I mean." She let out a loud sigh. "I just feel stuck, like I don't have any control over anything anymore."

"Hmm. That has to be frustrating. I'm sorry, Love."

"It's not your doing."

There was a long pause between them, then Cy broke the silence. "You want to come by the club? There's hardly anyone here right now. You can get on stage, take out your frustration on a pole."

Sheila snorted. What a ridiculous idea. She was waiting for Cy to start laughing, but she never did. "You can't be serious."

"I'm dead serious. The ladies say it's great for what ails ya. Plus, I bet you would look smoking hot twirling that thang in a circle."

"Oh, my god! You really want your vintage girlfriend to twerk on a pole?" Sheila was shocked and amused, unaware of what she'd said.

"You're my girlfriend, eh?" Cy's voice had slipped into a lower register with edge and gravely notes to it.

"I mean...I didn't mean to assume." They hadn't yet discussed what they were, although Sheila had made it clear she preferred to date one person at a time and for the person she was seeing to be on the same page as her.

"Come by the club. I want to give my girlfriend a nice, deep kiss."

Sheila pictured Cy biting the bottom edge of her lip, an action she often did when she was thinking intensely about something. When she did that while wearing her readers, it was absolutely hot. "I'll be there in fifteen."

• • • •

The Lounge in the daytime looked exactly like its name. A casual, chill spot with a deluxe bar. The side stages were set further back, and semi cloaked by sleek partitions. Sheila stood at the bar for only a few seconds before Cy came from the back. She was wearing a black cotton blazer and the most form fitting jeans Sheila had ever seen. Mouth slightly agape, Sheila outright ogled her, pleased with her decision to come by if only to get a look at those denim clad thighs.

"You look yummy," Sheila whispered in Cy's ear as they embraced. Her mood had slipped immediately into something more conducive to ear biting and innuendo once Cy was within reach.

Cy's cheeks bloomed like apples, and she could do nothing but grin for a few seconds before introducing Sheila to the bartender, Marla.

"Nice to meet you, Sheila. Know that we're all happy about this." Marla pointed a finger back and forth between Sheila and her boss. "She's more generous with days off since you two started seeing each other."

"Oh, so I'm good for morale, huh?" Sheila playfully pinched Cy's arm.

"Marla, you're fired." They all laughed, and Marla went back to wiping down bar glasses and stocking for the night.

"You're cute when you're a little embarrassed." Sheila let her hand wander to Cy's backside. She was feeling brazen and naughty.

"Would you like to see my office?"

"Mmhmm." Sheila delighted in the feel of Cy's hand clutching hers as she led her through the club towards the back. There was a short flight of stairs connected to a perch. On one end was an elevator and on the other end was a door.

"We call it the tower. It's a bit of a mess."

The office was pristine to Sheila's eyes. Not an invoice or pen out of place from what she could see. A corner desk sat beneath a row of monitors surveilling the club in its entirety. She could read the labels off the liquor bottles. The cameras were so sharp and clear. No wonder she was able to pick Sheila out of the crowd.

Another desk jutted out from the wall with a wire inbox and laptop on it. There were a couple of leather bucket seats and a table beside the wall of filing cabinets and a watercooler. Earpieces and walkies sat on chargers designated for security use on a shelf on the back wall near a door that looked to lead out to another hallway.

Sheila turned to face Cy having seen enough of the so-called mess. "I was under the impression I was going to get an official girlfriend kiss." She wrapped her arms around Cy's neck and pulled her close as the door clicked shut behind them.

"I do recall that being mentioned." Cy licked her lips, dipped her head, and teased Sheila with a light press of her lips until Sheila pressed back. Teasing the corners of her mouth with the tip of her tongue, Cy gave a little more, while keeping their bodies in contact. They walked toward the empty desk until Sheila's thighs met the edge and Cy lifted her onto it. She deepened their kiss, easing her tongue into her wet, hot mouth until she was moaning and clutching for her to get even closer.

Sheila found her hands eager to explore and let them roam from Cy's hips up to her lower back and down again until she discovered the firm cheeks Cy's jeans showcased. She squeezed, pulling their bodies even closer.

Cy smiled against her lips and continued kissing her, slowly, and methodically. She dribbled kisses over her chin and down her neck.

The door opened. "Hey, Cy, we need a signature for the...Sorry!" The door shut immediately, and they heard a female voice say, 'oh shit!' on the other side of the door, then footsteps hurriedly walking away.

"Mmm," Cy rested her forehead against Sheila's. "We shouldn't do this here," she said, sneaking another kiss.

"We got a little carried away, I guess." Sheila kissed Cy's bottom lip and sucked it until a semi-permanent pout formed. "But the good news is I do feel a teensy bit better." She pinched her fingers close together to show how much better she felt, but Cy took her hand and brought it close to her mouth, teasing her palm with her warm breath before sucking the tip of her index finger unabashedly. Sheila felt herself twitch between her legs. She squeezed her muscles until the sensation passed. "Would you like to come over tonight?"

"What time?"

"How about whenever you're done here?"

Cy nodded slowly. "Couple of hours tops." She tilted Sheila's chin towards hers and placed a very slow, deliberate kiss against her lips. They both felt the electricity pass from one to the other and had a hard time breaking apart.

Sheila made her way back down the stairs to the front of the club. She waved goodbye to Marla who was still stocking and cleaning the bar. When she got in her car Sheila sat for a few minutes thinking. Should she try to prepare dinner and make a whole thing of it or would Cy think less of her if she welcomed her into her warm desire right when she arrived? From those kisses Cy was planting on her she seemed to know what was in store. They both wanted to explore each other and find pleasure tonight. Encouraged, she made a plan and made her way toward her house with a stop along the way.

Nerves and anxiety started to turn her thoughts into attacks. She didn't have to think so much when she was married. Kharla got as good as she gave, but there was a sort of shorthand between them that had taken time to develop. Sheila wished she had someone to call, to talk out the nervous energy with while she got ready. But at the same time it was different than a conversation about what shoes to wear on a date. She couldn't call Kelly. Especially after how short she was earlier in the day. Darcy already thought it strange she and Cy hadn't crossed this bridge already. Sheila didn't want to get into a big debate about it while she was trying to channel her inner seductress. She'd just have to trust her instincts and feelings tonight. Cy was a gentle, understanding woman, right? Right. They'd been seeing each other for months, long enough to be comfortable and considerate to one another. Nothing untoward would happen.

Chapter 10

One hour and fifty-four minutes exactly after she left the club Sheila's doorbell rang. She'd showered and dressed casually, comfortably in a cropped sweatshirt and shorts after a stop at the grocery store and pharmacy. She couldn't host without at least having something on hand. They would both be satiated in as many ways as possible tonight. She hoped.

Cy had made a stop too, by the looks of it. The decision to dress casually and comfy was a mutual one. Her tee shirt and jeans clung to her frame, and she carried a small black nylon bag with her.

"Am I late?"

"Right on time." Sheila reached for her hand and brought her inside. The feel of Cy's thumb brushing back and forth in her palm reignited what they'd started at the club. Her entire body felt like she was being plucked, one section at a time. "I feel like we should...talk first, or I should offer you a glass of water or something."

Cy nodded, keeping her expression neutral. "I just need to say two things, then maybe you'll feel confident in showing me to your bedroom." She tilted her head and smiled a hesitant smile. "One, I know we've been abstinent for longer than maybe we needed to be and...I'm a little nervous." Cy toyed with her bottom lip. "Two, I want nothing more than to satisfy you tonight."

A little sound got caught in Sheila's throat. She felt her mouth go dry. Every drop of moisture in her body was rerouting south. She pulled Cy forward and pivoted on her heels with Cy in tow, leading her to the bedroom. There was no reason to say anything more about it.

She took the bag from her hand and set it at the foot of the bed, then prompted Cy to sit while helping her out of her shirt. It was a pleasure to look, to drink in the sight of Cy without pretense. Her smooth brown skin atop taut, lean muscle enticed and called to be touched.

Once her gaze had been satisfied, Sheila kissed Cy on the forehead, then planted kisses down the bridge of her nose and across her cheeks. She felt Cy nipping at her throat and ear, her tongue lashing her skin hungrily. Sheila gave in and kissed Cy's lips, eliciting a moan from her that came from somewhere deep. They stayed there, savoring the taste of each other until a need for more gripped them both. Sheila climbed on the bed, straddling Cy's lap. She balanced just so as Cy buried her face between her breasts, her hands following the slope of her back as she rocked slowly back and forth.

Sheila ran her fingers through Cy's hair, then pulled her head back. She wanted to look in her eyes as the pressure built. There she saw the restraint thinning, transforming into something more passionate, more wild than she'd ever known. For a second Sheila was afraid. But the emotion passed as soon as she felt the sweep of Cy's thumb over her nipple. She steeled herself against the urge to crumble from the direct touch. She wanted it again and again. Cy knowingly obliged, bringing her other hand into play.

It was a pleasure on the verge of torment. The more Cy toyed with each rigid tip, swiping and pinching, the harder they became and the harder they became the more Sheila's clit pulsed, aching for the same attention.

"Cynthia," she groaned, her breath ragged and labored. She caught a glimpse of mischievous delight in Cy's eyes.

The sound of shoes hitting the floor registered, but only after she realized Cy was standing with her still astride and then she was being gently placed on the bed. She reached for the button of Cy's jeans and tugged until it released, revealing the waistband of her under shorts.

"Take these off." Sheila tugged at the jeans, then lay back and removed her cropped sweatshirt. Her breasts buoyant and proud, beckoned for more attention.

Calculated and determined, Cy took her time shedding her jeans. Her eyes watched Sheila's reaction to every move she made. She crawled toward Sheila, riveted by the manipulation she applied to her breasts as she waited impatiently for contact. With slightly shaking hands she traced a line over Sheila's stomach, up and down, back and forth creating paths of goose bumps over the planes of her body.

Sheila put a stop to all the teasing. She took Cy's hand and guided it to the waistband of her shorts. "Please."

Cy slipped her fingers beneath the waistband, meeting moist curls. She took her time, letting her fingers acquaint themselves with Sheila's folds all the while watching and studying Sheila's stuttered breaths and the way her hips moved into her touch. "You're unbelievably wet, Sweetheart." Cy stroked over her damp lips, pursuing and probing without breaking entry while Sheila writhed beneath her. "Do you want me inside you?"

"Ohh." Sheila gripped the comforter between her fingers, unable to control her hips. "Yes...Yes, Cy, please."

Cy accommodated Sheila's request fully, filling her with one, then two fingers while stroking her clit, driving her deeper and deeper toward bliss.

Sheila felt herself clenching toward release. She rode the wave up, up, up until she was crashing and coming. Her limbs trembled on the way back down, but Cy was there talking her through it.

"That's it. I'm right here, Sweetheart." Cy covered Sheila's body with her own and let her find her way back to the present. "How's that?"

Sheila's voice was lost to the resounding pleasure still. She turned to Cy and nuzzled against her cheek. Finding the use of her hands again, she caressed Cy's shoulder with a light touch and applied kisses wherever she could reach.

"Was that okay?" Cy elongated her neck to feel the full extent of Sheila's lips, then cupped her face between her hands.

"That was...brilliant. I fear you've ruined me for any other."

"Good, 'cos I won't give you up easily."

Finding her strength, Sheila claimed Cy's lips again and gently pushed her onto her back. She peppered hot, open mouth kisses that turned into toothy bites across her chest and stomach. At the top of her shorts, Sheila rested the tips of her fingers and folded down the edge just enough to expose her mons. Sheila looked up as Cy cleared her throat, but she quickly closed her eyes, breaking their connection.

"Is this the part where you're nervous?" Sheila tilted her head, looking down over Cy's gorgeous frame sweetly. "You don't like to be teased, do you?"

"Mmm." She rested her head back and blew out a slow breath. Cy reached for Sheila and laced their fingers together. "I guess turnabout's fair play."

With her free hand Sheila squeezed her thigh, trying to ground her in the space. "You're safe. I promise." Giving up control was going to be hard for her. Sheila understood. She wanted Cy to feel just as comfortable as she'd been letting go. A little patience, a little encouragement should help her relax. "What's in the bag?" She thought a distraction could alleviate some of her angst.

Another shaky breath left Cy's body. She cleared her throat again. "Safety essentials."

Sheila smiled, reaching for the bag. "I made a stop too. I didn't know what we'd need." That seemed to ease a bit of Cy's apprehension. "Ooh, that's interesting," Sheila said, turning her head sideways and reviewing what she found inside the bag. She placed lubricant and a small vibrator on the bed. "Get comfortable."

Cy swallowed hard but did as she was told. She shimmied out of her shorts, grabbed a pillow, stuffed it beneath her head, and waited.

Sheila opened a square plastic pouch from the bag and blew across the top to make it pucker open. From inside she pulled out a dental dam and unfolded it while holding eye contact with Cy. Rising on her knees, Sheila hovered over Cy with the protective square. She dragged the silky, cool latex sheet across her stomach, then back up and over one of her nipples.

"Lick it." Sheila held it out in front of Cy's mouth while she moistened her own lips with the tip of her tongue. The immediate compliance turned her on. She quickly disappeared between her legs and placed the barrier. With all the sighing and moaning going on at the head of the bed, Sheila didn't think she'd have to do too much to get the desired result she was looking for. Still, she turned her full attention to Cy, bathing her in warmth and the steady pressure of her tongue, bringing out her most unencumbered self.

"Ooh..." Cy sucked in her breath over and over. She whimpered and writhed beneath Sheila's ministrations. Her body gave way to the pleasure one flexed muscle at a time, arching and cresting almost as soon as Sheila's fingers circled her vulva. Cy tucked her face in the crook of her arm, catching her breath and letting the tremors subside before she dared opening her eyes.

Sheila crawled up the bed and wrapped her arms and legs around her. She placed a kiss on her temple and held her close. A sense of protectiveness washed over her. How good it felt to be fully vulnerable with her and to have her trust in return. "Mmm." A soft final moan vibrated in her throat as she nuzzled closer and drifted off to sleep.

• • • •

Upon waking Sheila found Cy's leg thrown across her thighs. It was comforting and cozy, but at the same time hindered her from getting up. She lifted Cy's leg off her and slid out of bed. Her robe wasn't in any of the usual places, so she scurried to the bathroom naked, hoping she'd left a shirt or something in there to wrap up in.

A pair of sweats and a tee she'd thrown across the top of the hamper from the other morning still smelled clean enough to wear again. She slipped into the clothes and stretched. After using the bathroom and brushing her teeth she wondered if Cy would want something more comfy to slip into when she woke up. She shuffled back to the bedroom to lay out clothes, but Cy wasn't in bed. The clock on the dresser showed it being after ten. Sheila went back to the living room and continued to the kitchen when she didn't see Cy anywhere.

There in the kitchen she was posted up in front of the refrigerator crunching on a pickle spear from the end of a fork and searching for sustenance. She looked like a print underwear ad as she leaned and munched, her toned muscles flexing.

"Are you hungry?" Sheila strutted into the kitchen and opened her mouth for a bite of pickle.

"I'm starved."

"Not surprised. You put in some good work earlier." Sheila felt playfully satiated, but knew sex alone wasn't enough. "I'll make you a snack." She took the jar of pickles from Cy's hands, setting it on the counter before slipping her salty tongue in Cy's mouth and swayed.

"Mmm," Cy picked up the playful energy and gripped Sheila's rear end. "A nice enough little snack and I'll put in for overtime." She then held Sheila close for a deeper kiss. When they pulled a part, Cy looked contemplative. "You're, uh…the first woman I've been with in a really, really long time. I didn't anticipate it being so—" She rubbed the back of her neck while she searched for the right word.

"Intense, satisfying, restorative?"

"Mmhm. All of that and more." Cy cupped Sheila's chin. "I'm glad we waited."

"Me too." Sheila briefly wondered what the story behind Cy's self-restraint was all about, but she didn't ask. She busied her hands with preparing their snack.

The charcuterie was coming together. They each prepped the board Sheila set out on the countertop, feeding each other slices of cheese and apple, bits of shredded meat and olives in between kisses and ear licks. Sheila kept stealing glances at Cy. She was in no way uncomfortable with nudity, but Cy's state of partial undress was distracting her. "Baby, you are more than welcome to roam as you are, but I can't be responsible if your nipples get mistaken for delicacy." Sheila cupped one of Cy's breasts and lifted it towards her lips where she gently suckled.

"Ooh, woman! You're so deliciously wicked." Cy stole another quick kiss before strutting off to find something to cover up in.

Sheila finished loading up the charcuterie board in hopes of a little picnic on the couch with the tv on for background noise. She noticed the doorbell camera was blinking. Was someone outside? At this hour?

She clicked the image on her tablet to see if someone was really there. On occasion a fat enough bee or moth had set off the notification system.

Instantly her blood ran cold. All the good serotonin she'd just worked up drained from her body. She just stood at the edge of the living room staring at the uninvited guest on her porch. This had Momma Joyce all over it. She had to have shared her address with Kharla. There was no other explanation for her ex-wife to be standing outside her home. Sheila rushed to the door. She didn't want this to ruin the rest of her night with Cy.

"Leave!" As soon as she opened the door the fury of the last sixteen months exploded out of her. Sheila didn't waste any time growling out her directive. She didn't want there to be an iota of confusion that Kharla could spin into her being welcome.

"Baby, I need you right now. It's my mom. She's in the hospital." Kharla looked like crap. Worry lines ran across her ashened forehead, her eyes were puffy. She looked like she hadn't slept in days.

"I don't care." Sheila held firm. Through barred teeth Sheila let Kharla know flat out she wasn't welcome at her home. "You and your conniving mother need to stay away from me. I'm not your baby, I'm not your anything! You come back here, and I *will* call the police. Leave!" Sheila didn't give Kharla any time to plead her case. She shut the door and reset the alarm and tried to reclaim her calm, relaxed disposition, but she could feel herself shaking from head to toe.

"I hope it's okay that I'm wrapped up in this." Cy re-entered the living room wearing Sheila's floral robe. "This is the softest material I've ever felt in my life." She rubbed the sleeve against her face and walked across the floor. "Watch this," she spun around like she was a member of the *Temptations*. The bell sleeves and bottom billowed out like a cloud around her; She looked absolutely exuberant, beaming from the grandiosity of her movement.

Sheila smiled harder than she probably needed to, but Cy looked so happy and relaxed. She didn't want her to know anything was wrong. She didn't want her to know that Kharla had come to the house or that her mother-in-law was handing out her address like church mints. She didn't want her past to get any closer than it already was and ruin this for her. She would do anything to keep that from happening.

Chapter 11

Sheila spent the next day cleaning house and doing laundry. After coffee, Cy had to meet up with her friend Sonnie. He'd been tracking the black car, but without a clearer image or a vin number or something more, he was coming up empty.

Sheila hadn't seen the black car or anyone else suspicious in her neighborhood in weeks, so she was surprised Cy was still pursuing it. Sheila thought she just wanted some space after their sleepover with how fast she exited, which she didn't mind at all. She was glad Cy had left without lingering. She'd needed a little space herself. Her head was full of Kharla and Momma Joyce and she didn't know how much longer she could keep up the façade that everything was alright.

After she took two loads of laundry down to the basement, Sheila called St. Luke's for information on Momma Joyce. She assumed that's where she would be, but she hadn't given Kharla the chance to tell her.

"St. Luke's Medical Center. How can I help you?"

"Hi, I was calling about a patient that may have been admitted in the last twenty-four to forty-eight hours. Joyce Murphy."

"Are you family, ma'am?"

Sheila shut her eyes tight. As much as she was concerned about Momma Joyce she really just wanted to know if Kharla was telling the truth or making up some story to get her attention. "I'm her daughter-in-law."

The person on the other line hesitated. "We usually reserve information for immediate family only. You understand."

"Yes. I do. But I'm just trying to help my...My husband keep it together. He's away on business and he's...He's his mom's only...Any information would be a real help. He can take it if I tell him." Sheila wasn't about to go into the lesbian saga that was her life with some stranger over the phone. She just wanted to know if Joyce was there or not.

Another beat passed before the woman on the other end offered any details. "Ms. Murphy is stable. She's being monitored for cardiomyopathy, so she'll be here for at least a few more days."

"Thank you so much." Sheila ended the call. For whatever reason she was relieved that Kharla hadn't lied. It didn't change the fact that she'd just shown up at her house expecting her to be a shoulder to lean on. As for Momma Joyce, she'd have to answer for herself soon enough it seemed. Sheila tried not to let her feelings for Joyce overwhelm her. The old woman had betrayed her trust after all. *Obviously runs in the family,* she thought.

Sheila wondered how all of this must be affecting her former father-in-law, John. He was a quiet man, but reliable. He was probably worried and scared for his wife's health and trying to keep it together for Kharla, who, after last night, Sheila was reminded could get worked up and act out rather easily. Sheila picked up the phone to call John, to see how he was doing, but she just sat on the couch frozen. She didn't know what to say.

The rest of the morning felt like a bust. With laundry mostly folded and the kitchen floor mopped, Sheila struggled to keep herself busy. She was too sore to go for a walk and didn't fancy anything on tv. She turned to reading but couldn't concentrate for more than a few minutes at a time. *So much for making the most of my research summer,* she thought. So far, she'd dealt with family problems, gotten a stalker, and started dating amidst it all.

At least there's that, she thought. If someone had asked her a year ago how she imagined her life looking, this certainly wouldn't have been what she'd have described. But, all things considered, she was doing...alright. This wasn't the first time her life had hiccups, and she could do what she always did when things got hard, what she was taught. *Be the bigger person, be bigger than all of it!*

After lunch the plan was to go down to the hospital and just check on Joyce. She wanted to, as Joyce had said to her, put eyes on her, get a feel for how she really was doing. But as soon as she stepped onto the CCU floor she thought it was a mistake. What if Kharla was there? Or John? It was almost guaranteed they would be. Those two didn't play about Momma Joyce.

Sheila followed the heart arrow decals to the nurse's station. All the noise seemed counterproductive to a healing environment. The sound of people coughing, machines beeping, and constant announcements in an almost pattern like rotation was enough to give Sheila the beginnings of a headache.

She got the room number from the charge nurse and started walking in the direction of Joyce's room. The thought of seeing Joyce hooked up to machines made her stomach dip. The thought of seeing Kharla made Sheila absolutely unsettled. She clenched her fingers into fists over and over.

Room 522N was in front of her. The door was open, but the curtain was pulled all the way around like a tight seal. She couldn't see underneath it either as it almost reached the floor.

Staring at the ugly seafoam green and purple diamond pattern, Sheila stood silently trying to keep her composure. She closed her eyes and let out a quiet breath.

"Joyce, it's Sheila. Are you awake?" She waited a beat before pulling the edge of the curtain back a little.

"Sheila? Come on in here."

Sheila stopped holding her breath. She wasn't fully prepared to see her mother-in-law on an oxygen tube, but she'd known it was a possibility. She smiled and stepped into the space further. "Hi, Joyce. I came as soon as I heard." *A little white lie didn't hurt.*

"Aww, bless your heart. I'm doing better now. John was worried."

"I bet." Sheila stood by the bed, holding Joyce's hand. She noticed patches of dry skin up and down her arms alongside the bandages where they'd obviously taken blood. She also noticed how frizzy her hair was; the plaits were fat and fraying at the ends. She usually wore a little cropped wig whenever she left the house. It must've been left behind. "How long they got you in here for?"

"Couple days I suppose."

"Well, you just rest. Let them take care of you."

"Mmhm." Joyce closed her eyes. That little bit of conversation had zapped her energy.

Sheila let Joyce rest and started tidying up the room. She found a tub of disinfectant wipes and started scrubbing down anything that looked like it got frequent use. Then she folded the blanket that was in the chair in the corner and placed the pillow on top of it. John must've been sleeping there.

"What you over there messing about with?" Joyce had dozed off but was alert upon waking. She shifted around in the bed trying to get comfortable then gave up.

"Just tidying up a little. I didn't want to bother you while you were sleeping."

"I wasn't sleep. Just resting my eyes."

"Okay," Sheila nodded her head while chuckling to herself. "Momma, do you need me to bring you anything from the house? Your bonnet or a nightgown or something?"

"John and Kharlatta are bringing me my things. They should be back soon, I think."

Sheila nodded, although the sense of impending chaos activated her reflux. Being there when they got back probably wasn't the best idea for Sheila, especially if Kharla was still on a tear, but she wasn't about to sprint out of the room and abandon Joyce either. Sheila could push down her own feelings for a little while longer.

She stepped over by the bed and straightened out the edge of the sheet that had twisted around a cord. "I could braid your hair for you if you want. Looks like they were in a rush and messed up your part, Momma."

That seemed to perk her up. A scalp rub and retwist wasn't something Momma Joyce had ever turned down.

"If you want to, Hon. It don't matter to me."

That was a *yes*. Sheila immediately started taking down her hair, taking her time, making sure to be gentle on her edges and any knots that may have developed from rubbing against the bare hospital pillow. Her hair was baby soft and thinning in spots, but still carried a nice curl pattern.

"My mama used to do our hair every Sunday," Joyce mused. She had closed her eyes again. Her head swayed just a little as Sheila ran her fingers through her hair. "I always fell asleep."

"Marianne used to braid my hair so tight. I hated it. One time I had blisters all around the edges of my scalp because she'd pulled my hair so much." Sheila remembered crying to her dad and threatening to cut off all her hair with clippers. Sheila shook the old memory away and continued braiding Momma Joyce's hair. She'd decided on two simple Dutch braids.

"Well, looky there!" Joyce smiled as she looked in the mirror on the edge of the rolling table. "I look like a princess."

"You are a princess."

Sheila looked up towards the door to see Kharla standing there smiling. She had an overnight bag and a sack of food from a fast-food place, Rudy's, they used to go to. She didn't make a big show about Sheila being there but smiled and gave her a little nod. Kharla came in and freed her hands.

"Looking good, Momma. I brought you a chicken salad from Rudy's, approved by the doc, and your nightgown."

"You remember my lotion? It's so dry in here."

"Yes, ma'am."

Sheila listened to them go back and forth for a bit, remembering how they'd be posted up in the living room of her old house watching *Murder She Wrote* reruns on the weekends while she worked on grading papers. She must have had a smile on her face because when she caught Kharla's eye she was smiling back at her.

"I'm gonna get out of here. Let you two eat and catch up. I'll come back, though, okay, Joyce? Maybe tomorrow." Sheila kissed Momma Joyce on the forehead and stepped toward the door.

"Sheila, wait a sec." Kharla was on her heels. She followed her out into the hallway and folded her arms over her chest. "Thanks for stopping by to see her. I know it probably made her day."

"Yeah, of course." Sheila nodded her head and looked over her shoulder as if someone was waiting for her.

"I can keep you updated if you want. They keep doing all these tests. Sometimes she's not in the room when I come and I...They were talking about moving her to a regular floor. It's a lot. I'm going out of my mind."

"Sure, sure. That should be fine. Just, um, text me, I guess. Look, I need to go." Sheila pulled her keys out of her pocket and put all her attention into locating her car key on the ring. "I'll be around."

Sheila took a couple steps down the hall, then realized she was going the wrong way. She walked back past Kharla with her hands in her pockets trying to appear calm, but inside she was screaming and running toward the elevator.

Sheila had only been home from the hospital a few minutes when the doorbell chimed. Through the doorbell camera Sheila saw a white lady in a gray delivery uniform holding flowers. She cracked the door open.

"Delivery for Sheila Hudson?"

"That's me." She opened the door a little wider.

"Someone is definitely thinking about you. Have a great day." The woman handed over a large bundle of three dozen pink topaz roses.

"Thanks." The clean, floral scent filled the immediate air around her, but Sheila shoved her face in the blooms and inhaled. They smelled sweet. She brought them over to the coffee table and looked for a card. Assuming they were from Cy. She hoped they were. The card was simple.

Even strong women need their hands held sometimes. -Cynthia.

Sheila buried her face in them again while she picked up her phone and dialed.

"Hello?"

"I just got your flowers. They are lovely and unexpected. Thank you."

"You're welcome," Cy said. "I've been thinking about you all day. I...I hope it didn't seem like I was trying to get outta dodge this morning. I really was running behind."

"You're in the clear. I wasn't worried."

"Okay, good, good." Cy let out a breath. "I'm heading over to my parents' house later to grab a generator. Do you want to meet up for a late dinner or something?"

"Mmm. If I'm honest, I'm exhausted. I cleaned the house from top to bottom today and I don't know if I have anything left."

"Raincheck, then."

"Sounds good. Thanks again for my flowers."

Chapter 12

Sheila rushed home to change. She should have been ready already. For the long weekend she and Cy were going away for a few days. It was dinner with the Fraisers, then a quick drive up to New York for three days of relaxation. They had tickets to a couple of shows and a reservation at La Mere Resort & Spa.

Sheila drummed her fingers over the steering wheel, humming along to *Gladys Knight & The Pips* as she waited for the light to change. If she took 5th street all the way down to Montessori, she could shave off five minutes, but it was already a quarter to five on a Friday and she didn't want to risk an accident.

Her dashboard lit up. Cy was calling. She thought about ignoring it, but knew she'd be pissed if the shoe were on the other foot. Sheila cleared her throat and pressed accept call on the console.

"Hey, Sweetheart. Where are you?"

"Don't be mad. I'm running so late. I got carried away with photocopying articles again. But I'm on my way. I just need to change clothes and grab my bag."

"Okay. Just drive safely. I don't want you getting hurt."

"I just know you strongly dislike being late. I don't like disappointing you."

"You could never. That's a promise. Let me know when you're five or so minutes out from yours and I'll be on the way."

"Will do. Bye."

Sheila couldn't quite reconcile how patient Cy was all the time. Not that she herself was habitually late or eager for an argument. But she was so forgetful as of late and could run a hot streak when she was pissed; her moods lately needed to be studied the way she was all over the place. It didn't sit lightly with Sheila the idea that she was disappointing Cy, even if Cy didn't know she was.

It wouldn't have been an issue if Sheila had been where she'd said she was. Albeit she *was* at the library photocopying articles, just not *when* she said she was.

That was much earlier. Right now she was coming from Momma Joyce's house like she'd been doing for the last week ever since she'd been released from the hospital. She'd wanted to help and spend time with Joyce and John. It started out as simply bringing a couple of ready-made meals to the house so John didn't have to cook and could keep Momma Joyce comfortable and in good spirits.

Then it turned into them telling stories until late in the evening while folding a basket of laundry or helping Joyce wash up. Occasionally she'd still be there when Kharla came over after work and they all would watch a little tv together.

It was all very pale in comparison to anything salacious or tawdry that could have been happening with an ex, but Sheila felt bad about it. Especially now that she was being strategic with her words and was grossly leaving out chunks of her day when asked. It had gotten out of hand, and she didn't even know why she hadn't just told Cy the truth.

She pulled up to her house and parked the car. "Shit!" She'd forgotten to let Cy know when she was five minutes away. She sent the text as she walked inside.

On my way.

Sheila grabbed her bag and set it by the door then ran back to the bedroom and grabbed her dress and boots and took them to the bathroom with her. She figured she had time for a quick rinse in the shower if she didn't primp.

She turned the shower on and pulled the curtain around the tub ready to get in but had to run to the bedroom again because she forgot to grab underwear and a bra. "Get it together, Sheila!" She quickly chastised herself and stepped into the shower.

Not two minutes had passed, and she was stepping out to the sound of the doorbell ringing and light knocking. She wrapped up in a towel and scampered out to see if it was Cy. It was her of course, prompt as usual.

"This doesn't look like ready," she laughed, grabbing at Sheila's towel.

"I'm trying. I thought I had time for a quick shower. I'll be ready in ten minutes tops. My overnight bag is by the door."

"Don't rush on my account." Cy shut the door and held Sheila in place by the ends of her towel as she'd started to walk away. "We can skip dinner altogether if you're on the menu." She lowered her head to kiss and bite at Sheila's neck.

Sheila giggled and pretended to squirm. "We've already canceled on Darcy and Edwin twice. We really should go tonight."

"If you say so." Cy released Sheila with a soft pat on the behind.

• • • •

"Chica! I haven't seen you in weeks!" Darcy greeted Sheila and Cy at the door of her craftsman home with arms outstretched.

"You look positively radiant," she whispered, pulling back from Sheila to get a full look at her. She gave Cy the once over then immediately gave Sheila the look of approval.

"Darcy, this is Cy Owens. Cy, my good friend and colleague Darcy Fraiser."

"So nice to finally meet you."

"Likewise. I've heard so much about you. Least of all how gorgeous you are. Sheila, you left out so many details." All three of them laughed and Darcy stepped aside to let them through the entryway.

"Eddie is out back finishing up on the grill. We thought since the weather has been nice, we'd sit out there."

"Girl, you know I don't do insects." Sheila made a face.

"I had Eddie set up the lamps and tiki torches. You'll be fine."

Cy took Sheila's hand and brought it to her lips as they traversed through the living room, past the kitchen, and out the back onto the patio.

"Look who I found." Darcy' sing-song voice rang out across the air as she brought them to the back yard and made introductions. "Cy this is my husband, Edwin. Eddie, this is Sheila's friend Cy."

"Nice to meet you." Edwin dapped Cy up awkwardly then went back to poking at the steaks.

Cy looked impressed by the grill. "Is this the Webber?"

"Yes, indeedy. You know your grills. I like that." Edwin smiled wide and started showing Cy some of its attributes.

Sheila and Darcy had stepped over to the bar.

"You didn't have this last time I was here. I love it." She surveyed the built-in ice chamber on the bar top and all the cubbies for various bottles and utensils. The stainless steel and mahogany looked so sleek together

"All Eddie's idea. I figured why not. He likes to entertain, he should have some gadgets of his own."

"It's nice." Sheila poured herself a glass of red wine and mixed a gin and tonic for Cy. She took in how the outdoor area flowed. The red stone pavers matched with the siding and added depth to the space as did the lantern lights spaced around the perimeter of the patio.

It definitely looked like a great deal of work had been put into it. She wondered if her small backyard could be transformed into a cute little spot to hang out with friends on occasion.

"You make plates too?" Darcy asked, her top lip curled up to the side when Sheila returned from handing off Cy's drink.

Sheila furrowed her brow. "What?"

"She can get her own." Darcy seemed to want to suggest something, but she was suddenly tight lipped.

"We have mutual respect for each other. I'd fix her a plate if we were at a shindig. It doesn't mean I'm submissive or putting her in a category. Or anything like that."

"Mmhm," Darcy sipped her wine. "But how do you figure out who does what? Doesn't it get confusing?"

Sheila laughed, drawing the attention of both Cy and Edwin. "Darcy, girl, stop. Cy is forty years old. She isn't the least bit confused about anything. Neither am I. You and little Eddie get confused because you don't communicate and navigating the world has been easy for you. *Easy!*"

"Sounds like it's getting heated over here. What are you two talking about, huh?" Cy now stood in the space left open by Darcy and Sheila's chairs. She sipped at her drink and casually rubbed the back of Sheila's neck.

"Just an age-old debate. Would you fix ya mans a plate? And if ya mans was a woman, what then?" Sheila rolled her eyes and shook her head all at once. She couldn't believe how Darcy was acting. Had she always felt this way?

"Well, I know Sheila can debate with the best of them, but tonight is about...I don't know what tonight is about. But I'm happy to be here with you." Cy pulled Sheila up out of her seat and set her drink down on the table. She twirled Sheila and managed a two-step of some sort that made them all perk up.

Edwin found the stereo remote and pressed play. Al Green started crooning through the speakers. Edwin came to Darcy's side and kissed the top of her head.

"Let's show these two how it's done." He took her hand and guided her to the edge of the patio where he could still keep an eye on the food.

Sheila and Cy were off to themselves, dancing close and gazing into each other's eyes.

"What was that all about?"

"Beats the heck outta me. I thought we were on the same page, then she made that comment when I brought you the drink." Sheila tucked her head against Cy's neck. "I swear I feel like I'm losing my mind."

"It's all good. I got you."

"Dinner is served!" Edwin clapped the tongs in the air like a dinner bell. "Steaks are medium, asparagus is buttered and garlic'd," he looked to Darcy to check if that was a word, then continued, "and the mac and cheese is ooey gooey!" The announcement did much to clear the air.

"Grilled mac and cheese, Edwin? What else can that thing do?" Cy was already eyeing the large casserole sized dish.

"The Webber is great for everything. You can flame on top, smoke with it, and bake. I don't ever have to leave my backyard."

The two grill aficionados kept the conversation going, talking about recipes and techniques they liked to use while Sheila shot daggers at Darcy from across the table. Was it the wine talking? Or had Darcy always been hostile towards her, and she'd not seen it? When everything with Kharla and the divorce was going down, Darcy had seemed so supportive. Sheila cut into her steak, wondering what she'd done to deserve the vitriol tonight. *Straight people.* She took a bite and chewed. The meat was tender and juicy. It melted like butter, like a memory washing over her. Sheila closed her eyes for a second. She was remembering. The one time Marianne had been nice to her, overtly kind, was when she was in the tenth grade. After practicing lines for the school play for weeks, Sheila was crushed when she didn't get the part. Marianne seemed absolutely thrilled, giddy to offer her comfort.

Sheila had another Marianne, in friend form, on her hands. She visibly shivered and rubbed her hands up and down her arms.

"Yeah, that's my special steak rub. It'll give you chills!" Edwin was too thrilled to see them all reacting to his cooking. There was a collective chuckle from the group at his joy over meats and rubs, but Cy was already shrugging out of her jacket. She draped it over Sheila's shoulders and brushed her cheek with her thumb.

Sheila mouthed a soft *thanks* and went back to eating while sneaking glances at Darcy. Their recent inability to get together and dish had been a blessing. Sheila knew she would have looked for a sounding board about her former in-laws and being around Kharla. That would have been all she needed to have Darcy making snarky comments about that situation tonight. Sheila looked around the table, trying to get out of her head. The stretched smile she gave Cy when she looked at her felt heavy and uncomfortable. An uneven mix of emotions fell over her. She needed to come clean about Kharla.

Chapter 13

Once they were in the car headed out of town Cy casually rehashed the night with the Fraisers. "That dinner was really good. Mac and cheese on a grill. I wasn't ready. I gotta talk to Pop about upgrading his grill. That Webber setup is sick."

Sheila half listened to Cy's review of the evening as they drove along the 118 toward I-80. The scenery flitted by as they sped down the highway. Sheila just watched, letting her eyes pick out shapes in the dark. The thought that maybe she should end things with Cy popped in and out of her mind. What really was the probability that she could make this work with her history?

She could eradicate all relationships altogether now and just grow old not having to worry about letting anyone down, or worse being let down. Shaking that thought clear from her head, she shifted in her seat so she could look at Cy before she spiraled further.

"You can go to sleep if you want. It's a couple hours still until we hit the state line."

"I'm okay for now. How are you? You good?" Sheila reached over and squeezed Cy's thigh who then took her hand and weaved their fingers together.

"I'm excited for our little getaway. It'll be nice to focus on us all weekend. Plus, I haven't been to New York in a minute."

"My school took us on a field trip believe it or not. Senior year. We saw *Phantom of the Opera*. That was back when I wanted to be a Broadway actress."

"You didn't pursue your dream of being in the theater? Why not?"

"Things changed. I realized I wasn't good enough." Sheila smiled weakly then closed her eyes and leaned her head against the headrest. She hummed along with the radio and took solace in the semi darkness of the car. "Hey, where did you get that line you had the florist put on the card when you sent me those roses? About strong women needing their hands held."

"It was something my mom used to say to me when I was going through a rough time. I don't know where she got it from, but I liked it. Made me feel like I could ask for help if I needed it." She shot a glance over at Sheila.

"I see how hard you work to make everyone around you happy and how you hold yourself together. You know you don't have to do it alone."

The back of Sheila's neck tightened; she squirmed a bit in her seat. It was awkward being seen so clearly. Sheila propped her head in her hand up against the car window and looked out. She felt awful. "What rough time," she asked.

"You really want to hear about it? It's not the most upbeat topic. I'd hate to bring down the mood."

"You don't have to tell me. It's fine."

"I was...um, I was in an abusive situation, an abusive relationship. It was the hardest time of my life." Cy shifted in the driver's seat and steered with one hand. She cleared her throat and kept her eyes on the road ahead.

"Cy, I'm so sorry. I...I wasn't expecting you to say that." Sheila let the silence take its course and thin out. "Is it...too hard to talk about?" Sheila reached over the center console and placed her hand lightly on Cy's forearm.

"It used to be. I'm not bringing it up at dinner parties, if that's what you mean. I've worked really hard to heal that part of me and still sometimes...I told you, this isn't really a car conversation."

Sheila was quiet, thinking about how anyone could do that to another person, someone they said they loved. She remembered how Cy's mom had asked her to be kind and respectful. Lydia had been there for her daughter throughout that episode in her life, no doubt.

"What's it like having such a supportive, loving mom? I've been remembering things about my mom through this new lens. Knowing that she resented me for straining her marriage. It puts an entirely different slant on things."

"I can't lie, it's nice. Knowing Lydia has my back and best interest in mind...Even when I'm dead wrong about something and she calls me to the carpet, I know she still cares about me."

The smile on Sheila's face was genuine. She was glad that Cy had a great connection with her mom, both her parents.

"She's not been blowing up your phone, has she? She's a talker."

"We've phoned a couple of times. There was an offer to teach me how to make coco bread. She said something about it being your favorite." Sheila tilted her head to look at Cy's profile. Even in the dark Sheila could see the chagrin on Cy's face.

"That's her way of trying to see how serious you are about me. I'm sorry. That woman has been trying to marry me off for a while now. I'll talk to her. Unless, you know..." The lights of oncoming traffic lit up Cy's face, putting her wide smile on display.

Sheila scrunched her nose up. The conversation was getting too heavy. *Marriage?* Why would she bring up marriage? Sheila cracked the window. She needed some fresh air.

"What is it? Are you feeling sick?"

"Hmm. I'm just...Hot flash." She fanned herself with her hand until she could breathe normally again. She felt like she was going to throw up, and the space behind her eyes pulsed with pain. Cy turned the circulation fan on high and pointed the vents in her direction.

"I can pull over at a rest stop if you need me to, Baby."

"No, no. I'll be fine. It'll pass. Just a hot flash. Wait 'til you start experiencing them." She could feel Cy periodically glancing over at her, concern written all over her face. Sheila closed her eyes. Everything felt out of whack, her body, her mind, her sense of control. She took a few more deep breaths. *You can get through this. Hold it together.*

• • • •

Sheila woke up as the car slowed, pulling up to the valet in front of the resort. She looked around and reckoned she'd dozed off the last half hour of the ride. Cy was grabbing their bags and coming around to the passenger side to offer her a hand out of the car.

They walked inside the resort together side by side looking like a cute unassuming couple. But in the reflection of the check-in desk Sheila only saw their distorted faces. She was withholding things from Cy, and it was only going to hurt her down the road. She'd promised she'd treat Cy with kindness and respect, and she'd manage to break that promise the first chance she got.

"Enjoy your stay, ladies."

"Thank you," Sheila said meekly, then followed Cy to the elevators.

"I'm going to take a shower when we get up to the room. I feel gritty."

"Yeah, okay." Sheila smiled and leaned onto the elevator rail. She couldn't shake the nagging feeling in her gut.

Once in the room Sheila stopped feeling guilty long enough to take in the sight of the deluxe suite they'd be staying in. It was floor to ceiling luxurious. A tad bit bridal meets brocade but luxurious, nonetheless. White marble with gold swirls etched along the edges traversed the floors disappearing, then reappearing throughout the suite.

Overstuffed furniture in rich maroon, gold, and green along with sheer movable curtains meant to create smaller spaces throughout made it seem like she was visiting with regal heiresses or some such. It was more than she deserved.

Sheila meandered through the room, running her hand over the plush fabric of the couches, trying to ground herself while Cy took their bags to the bedroom and stretched her back in the doorway.

"Quick shower, then we can relax, maybe have a nightcap. I want to walk around the city in the morning." Cy slipped out of sight, but her happy humming lingered in the background.

The double doors leading to the balcony caught Sheila's eye. She opened them and quickly stepped out to catch the night breeze. What could she even do at this point?

All weekend would be miserable if she walked around with a *fake it 'til you make it* attitude and it would be ruined from the start if she fessed up now. It wasn't fair to either of them. *Sheila,* she chastised, going back and forth with herself. Stepping out of her shoes onto the cool tile of the balcony soothed her as she prepared to rip the band-aid off and tell the truth about where she'd really been.

Cy found her still on the balcony. She'd taken up residence in one of the reclining lounge chairs and put her feet up, her eyes focused on the far distance.

"How about that nightcap?" She was dressed in silky pajama pants and a black halter camisole, a towel half draped around her neck while she used the other end to dry her hair.

Sheila made a little mewling sound in the back of her throat. Her heart ached in her chest like it was breaking.

"I need to tell you something," she started and pointed for Cy to sit across from her. It had to be obvious this wasn't a happy talk. Concern flashed across Cy's face as she sat, but it quickly dissipated as she prepared to listen.

"I...made a mistake. I lied to you." Sheila closed her eyes, rethinking this confession. She should have waited, but the cat was out of the bag now. "It was a lie of omission, no less a lie though. I'm sorry. It's just been eating me up and—"

"What did you omit?" Cy remained neutral, still open to listening according to her body language.

"I've been going...spending time with my former in-laws in the evening after going to the library. Joyce was recently in the hospital and John needed help with her. I don't know why I didn't just tell you."

Cy raised her eyebrows a little, but other than that Sheila couldn't tell what was going on in her head about what she'd just revealed. "Is that it?"

Here we go, Sheila thought. Her breath sounded loud as she blew out to steady herself. "Sometimes my ex-wife is there in the evenings."

Cy licked her lips and sat forward. She started to speak, then stopped herself. "Did something happen between you two?"

SHEILA ON THE MEND

Sheila shook her head. "No. She came to the house to tell me about Joyce the night you and I...I made her leave and made it clear she couldn't come around. But I went to the hospital to see Joyce and then...things just kinda snowballed into me going over there and..."

Cy stretched her legs out in front of her and steepled her hands on her lap. "I don't see that you did anything wrong. Please don't be upset about it."

Sheila felt a little relief. She couldn't wrap her mind around Cy's demeanor though. Did she even care?

"Anything else you need to get off your chest?" Cy offered her a kind smile.

"Don't do that. Don't smile at me like that."

That made Cy actually chuckle a little, then she had the good sense to reign it in. "I can't smile at you now? Sweetheart. I suspect you thought I was going to yell or get angry or something. That's not me." Cy pressed her lips together. "Yeah, I'm a little hurt, but I'm not gonna take that out on you. I don't think you're seeing the situation as clearly as you think you do."

Sheila clasped her hands together. She still wasn't sure of what was going to become of their relationship. She hadn't anticipated this alternative reaction. "What...How do we..." Sheila's head was starting to hurt, she could feel the tears welling up in her eyes, but she held them back

"On our first date I asked if you and your ex were done. That wasn't really fair." Cy cleared her throat and fidgeted with the hem of her halter while looking down. "I was trying to protect myself, but I didn't have all the information." Cy stood up and moved to the footrest in front of Sheila. She took Sheila's hands in hers. "When you talk about Joyce and John your face lights up. And no wonder, your own parents lied to you your entire life. Your mom takes digs at you for every little thing—can't wait to meet her by the way." Cy nudged Sheila's calf, trying to lighten the mood.

"You don't just see Joyce as a former in-law, she's a surrogate for the mother-daughter relationship you missed out on. I can deal with you being around Kharla if that gets you family time the way you need. I see the connective tissue there. Nurse it or sever it, it's up to you. I'll support that. I'll support you."

Sheila sniffled and wiped her eyes. "Thirty percent of this relationship is me crying on you." They both laughed.

"Come on," Cy led Sheila back inside by her shoulders. "Is this what you alluded to when you said you didn't want to disappoint me?"

Wiping her eyes with the back of her hand Sheila nodded.

"Like I said, you could never. Just talk to me. I'm pretty chill. Ask my people. You're not going to scare me away."

They hardly left the suite all weekend. Room service became very accommodating and responsive to their frequent calls. They relied heavily on the concierge as well.

"I guess we should go out and let the sun touch our skin." Sheila sat up from the floor pallet they'd made out of the couch cushions, blankets, and covers.

"It's raining." Cy lowered herself back down to the floor beside Sheila with two spoons in one hand and a pint of ice cream in the other.

"It is not. It's a breezy seventy-four degrees out. I checked the weather when you went to greet Paul at the door."

"I knew I should have taken your phone." She nestled in next to Sheila and unearthed the remote to the big screen from one of the cushions. "Think we can find *Rosa, Rosa!* on this thing?" Sheila was too involved with scraping the melted chocolate and caramel from the ice cream lid into her mouth.

"I don't think you're gonna find that, Babe. Let's watch something romantic. Preferably Black and with lesbians." She held out a bite of ice cream for Cy to taste.

"Mmm," Cy flipped through the channels looking for Sheila's request. "I don't think we're finding both. One or the other maybe."

"We could just make our own then." Sheila put the carton of ice cream on the table and took the remote out of Cy's hand while pulling her down toward the pillows.

Chapter 14

When they got back to Wilksberg late Monday afternoon Sheila didn't expect to find Kelly boo-hooing on her steps. The days she and Cy spent feeding each other and making love everywhere they could had cast a sort of lover's bubble around them. Nothing could touch them. But the very real world was waiting for them as soon as they stepped back to reality.

Cy was the first to notice Kelly sitting there like a lost puppy. She dangled Sheila's bag over her shoulder and sort of stood there trying to ascertain if the girl was a danger or just lost. "Do you know this woman?"

Sheila stopped short behind Cy and leaned around to see. "Kelly?"

Kelly looked up, wiping her nose with a nearly disintegrated tissue she'd been clutching, then stood up. "Where have you been? I've been calling." After a bout of loud wailing and semi hyperventilating Kelly blurted out, "I called off the wedding."

"Oh, shit, Kelly! We were away. I turned my phone off. Come inside."

"Hey, I'm Cy."

"I know. You're thicker than I remember." Kelly looked Cy up and down, still sniffling and dabbing her eyes. "No offense, I mean it in a nice way."

Cy looked unsure but smiled anyway. "Thanks."

Sheila managed to wrangle her keys out of her pocket and open the door with Kelly and Cy filing in behind her.

"Kelly, what happened? Start from the beginning."

"Well, your mother is what happened." Kelly curled her lips inward as if she were reliving when everything went to hell.

Cy appeared with a box of Kleenex then disappeared with Sheila's bag into the bedroom. When she returned, she went straight to the kitchen where she grabbed three bottles of water from the fridge and brought them over to the sitting area for Kelly, Sheila and herself.

"Thanks, Baby." Sheila turned back to Kelly and encouraged her to go on.

"That woman is a *beast!* A cruel, evil beast with a black heart from Satan himself."

"Sounds about right," Sheila said. Her attempt at levity wasn't appreciated. She rubbed Kelly's back and sat quietly so she could finish telling her story.

"She's moved herself into our house first off. She's a disgusting little slobette who can't mind her business. No wonder Braxton sent her packing."

Gasping, Sheila looked over her shoulder at Cy, eyes wide and mouth lolling open. This was the first she was hearing of any turmoil. "My dad kicked her out? What happened?"

"They are trying 'some time apart' is what Marianne said. But I see through her story. I bet Braxton's had enough of her. I certainly have. She criticizes every single thing I do. She got mad I didn't know what a milk pie was."

"Sounds disgusting whatever it is."

Kelly nodded and continued, shifting her eyes from Cy back to Sheila. "She said I wasn't good enough for Bryce. She said I needed to watch my back, Sheila. That old hag threatened me!" Kelly covered her mouth and gasped. "I'm sorry. I didn't mean to say that about your mom."

"Kelly, you're upset and...you're not wrong."

"What did Bryce say?" Cy was just as invested in Kelly's story. She'd crossed her legs and was leaning forward so as to not miss a word. This was like an episode of the telenovela.

Kelly crumpled again. The entire contents of the Kleenex box practically occupied her hands. "He didn't. He didn't say a word in my defense. He lets her walk all over me." Kelly sobbed and fell into Sheila's arms.

The crying went on for upwards of an hour. Sheila and Cy kept looking at each other, but Kelly didn't seem eager to leave the cradle of comfort Sheila provided. When Kelly excused herself to the bathroom Sheila and Cy both made exasperated sounds.

"I've got to call my dad. I can't believe he put Marianne out."

"Your brother didn't defend his fiancée? What kind of sorcery is your mom working with?" Cy bit her lips. "I'm sorry. I shouldn't have intoned that your mom is a witch."

Again, Sheila didn't feel compelled to defend her mother. "You're not wrong, though." The sigh she let out rattled with frustration as she fell back onto the couch. "I think I should stay in with Kelly tonight. See if I can't make her feel any better."

Nodding in agreement, Cy stood up and stretched. "Yeah, she's going to need all your help dealing with your mom if she gets back with Bryce. I'll call you later?"

"Yes, please." Sheila was up and walking with Cy towards the door.

"Okay." Cy placed a kiss on Sheila's forehead and turned to leave.

"Love you." With her hand on the doorknob, Sheila stopped and cocked her head to the side once she realized what she'd said.

Her slow blinks couldn't make her rewind or take back what she'd said. "Um, you know what I mean."

Cy spun around, her mouth agape and eyes dancing. She had a smile as wide as the Ohio River was long. "No takebacks," she said, slowly shaking her head. "No takebacks." She placed a soft kiss on Sheila's lips while gently stroking her cheek.

Once Cy was gone Sheila blew out a giant puff of air and returned to the couch. She hadn't meant to say that, but she hadn't *not* meant to say it either. It was one of those things. When you're so comfortable with someone what you're thinking just comes out. It felt good seeing Cy's reaction to hearing it. She didn't freak out. A good sign. Rubbing her thumb back and forth over her bottom lip, Sheila let the feeling sink in. She bristled at the idea for a bit, but it was obvious. She was falling in love again. "Oh, boy!"

Sheila was still on the couch when Kelly came out of the bathroom. She'd pulled her hair back into a ponytail and taken her makeup off. She looked like a toy that had been left out on the sidewalk in the rain. She sniffled her way back over to the couch and plopped down.

"What am I going to do, Sheila?"

"Well, for starters you're going to stop crying. I mean you can cry if you want to but give yourself a break. Your head has got to be pounding. Take some deep breaths and try not to worry. Bryce is a fool and so is his mother if they think you're going to put up with their nonsense."

Sheila popped up and went to the kitchen. She came back with a pint of caramel banana ice cream, pretzel rods, and two spoons. "Second, you're gonna eat some of this ice cream and listen to what I found out a few weeks ago about Marianne's affair."

From the look on Kelly's face, it was evident she'd stopped thinking about her problems for the time being. Her face contorted with devilish glee when she heard those words. Her long fingers reached for a spoon, ready to listen.

• • • •

Dishing the dirt on her mother felt good after years of her mistreatment and it seemed to do the trick for Kelly's mental state as well. She was full of questions and theories of her own as to who Sheila's biological father was.

"What if he's someone famous? Like, what if your dad is Lou Rawls?"

"Lou Rawls!" Sheila fell back on the couch. She was beside herself, laughing so hard she almost burst into tears. "How did you come to that choice?"

"Hear me out. He's old enough, he's a ladies' man, you know how much your mom loves her some baritones, and he used to play Pittsburgh all the time."

Sheila pursed her lips and craned her neck as if to say that was no real evidence. "How do you know he played Pittsburgh all the time? Cite your sources."

"Okay, I made that last part up, but could you imagine?" They both broke out into uncontrollable laughter again, swatting at each other lightly out of the absurdity of their conversation.

Once the laughter died down and they were spent, Kelly turned to Sheila. "It doesn't make it right, how she treated you growing up, but holding a secret like that...I see how it must've turned her into such a self-loathing, hateful person. You didn't deserve any of that. I don't deserve it either."

"No, you don't." Sheila got up from the couch and stretched. "Okay, girlie, do you want to stay over? I've got extra linens on top of the dryer. We probably need to eat some real food too."

"You get the linens, and I'll order from Tikka Hut."

"And that is why you're the best sister!"

"Aww, you still want to be sisters?" Kelly's voice trembled a little. "Even if I don't marry your brother?"

"Especially if you don't marry that goblin. He may be related to me by blood, but I choose you. You've been a spectacular friend to me, and I cherish that."

Kelly got up to hug Sheila and then they each pursued their respective duties to carry on with the evening. In the basement Sheila noticed the weatherstripping on the small window flapping. Was there air getting in? She pulled the step stool over to the window for a closer look.

There was a break in the seal. Fixing that would be easy. Braxton had taught her how ages ago. But upon closer inspection there appeared to be fingerprints on the glass. Looking closely, she also noticed footprints on the ground directly outside the basement window. A bit of dread rose up in her chest. The basement window area was inside the fence. It was hardly visible to the unknowing eye. She feared someone had been in her yard. Even though she hadn't seen the black car for weeks Sheila felt confident it had something to do with that. It wasn't a coincidence. The stalker was back.

A strip of duct tape held the remaining seal in place for now. After putting the boxes with the Christmas ornaments directly below the window like a booby trap and grabbing the linens for Kelly, Sheila went back upstairs. She had a new list of things she needed to do. Starting with getting a call with Cy's friend Sonnie.

He had to know something more than what he'd relayed to Cy. Or at least he had to have a way of finding out.

Chapter 15

The alleyway between Serenity Blvd and Sycamore Street was so narrow Sheila thought she might have a panic attack. Clinging to Cy's arm while gripping the satchel with her laptop in it, she scooted along the wall and practically bumped into Cy when she stopped walking abruptly.

"Why are we here, Cy? It smells like urine." Looking over her shoulder, Sheila felt like she was being watched. She observed Cy's calm, cool, collected demeanor and thought she'd either been here before or she was going to trade her for something illegal.

"It's fine," Cy said casually. "And, yes, we are most definitely being watched." Cy felt around the brick wall with her hands like she expected to find something there hidden among the mortar.

"What are you doing? I don't understa—"

A small slot in the wall, just large enough for someone to look out, opened up. Sheila gulped when two brown eyes appeared, looking from side to side.

"What's the password of the day?"

"Calamari," Cy said. She looked over her shoulder at Sheila and winked.

The slot closed with a slap. There was a click followed by a low buzz, then what appeared to be a hinged storm drain grate popped open.

"It's dark at first, so step slowly." Cy opened the grate and guided Sheila down into the ground. After stepping down after Sheila, she closed the grate behind them. "Stay to the right."

"What is this?"

"You said you wanted to talk to Sonnie."

"Not like a cold-war spy, Cynthia." Sheila was whispering through tight, angry lips while trying to find her way in the dark. "Are we doing something illegal?"

"No." Cy paused for a second. "Well, I don't think so."

"Oh, my god."

Sheila's under breath grumbling made Cy laugh. They were walking into a room that had more light than the entryway. There was used restaurant furniture stacked up in the corners and an empty convenience store cooler sat unused against the wall.

"What is this place?' Sheila stood as close to Cy as possible while scanning for rodents. They were in a tunnel beneath the city. Three arches lead to different corridors and the sound of electricity hummed amid the sound of an industrial fan. It was steamy down there.

Cy pulled out a little card with a map on it from her jacket. "I always get a little turned around down here..." She drifted off looking at the map. "To the right. This way."

They walked about 300 feet then turned again and stopped at a fireproof door. Cy did a special knock that sounded a lot like *Rapper's Delight.*

The door opened a crack and a man with blue cornrows and a goatee poked his head out. When he saw Cy, he opened the door a little wider so he could eyeball Sheila. A slick little side smile opened up his face. "That's you, right there, huh?" He was nodding and grinning by the time he'd given Sheila the once over. "Come in. Close the door."

Sheila wrapped her arms around her waist. When she breathed out, she saw her breath. Several computer monitors and stations lined the back wall next to a superhub wired into at least ten machines. That explained the temperature, but Sheila still couldn't wrap her mind around this place or Sonnie at first glance. He was wearing an open Hawaiian shirt over a plain white tee and blue jeans. He wore gold rings on all fingers of both hands.

Sonnie walked back over to the larger-than-life computer monitor and sat down at his desk. He hit three keys, and the monitor displayed an image of Cy and Sheila standing on the sidewalk in front of her house.

"Holy shit...Who is this guy?"

"He's the best." Cy pointed at the monitor, giving the kill sign.

Sonnie took the image down and posted another one. The black car. "I ran into so much gobly gook trying to put a name to this vehicle. They are resourceful, that's for sure. With no VIN it's been a bit of a bust"

"Were you able to find anything?" Sheila was still over by the door taking in the room. There was a stack of Blacksploitation VHS tapes stacked on top of a filing cabinet next to a box of auxiliary cords and chargers.

"Of course." Sonnie waved her over. "Look right here." He zoomed in on the decal on the rear passenger side window.

"What is that?"

"It's a Mill-Amherst parking sticker." Sonnie looked at Cy on the left of him and Sheila on the right.

"Oh..." Sheila hadn't expected the car to lead back to the college. Her stalker could be any of the student body, a colleague, someone she'd worked with closely for months or for a day. The room dipped and she started to sway.

"There's a little barcode on the side. I was able to run it."

"So, we know who this weirdo is?" Cy had crossed her arms over her chest and leaned back.

"Not exactly. Mill-Amherst only keeps parking records for about five years, then they overwrite the sticker codes and reuse them. This one isn't active. The last person I've got on record for this sticker is Belinda Johnston."

The name didn't ring a bell for Sheila. "Will the footage on my laptop give us any other clues?"

"I doubt it. The camera isn't designed for long range. But I was able to hac—"

Cy cleared her throat loudly to get Sonnie's attention. When he looked over, she closed her eyes and shook her head.

"I was able to gain access to a couple of surveillance cameras the city installed. One is about a mile away and the other one is on a fake tree a mile in the other direction." Sonnie worked to pull up the feeds.

"You…gained…access…to a city installed camera?" Sheila shot a look over at Cy and raised her eyebrows. *I thought you said this wasn't illegal.* The tilt of her head conveyed the message that they would discuss this later.

Sonnie glossed over Sheila's question like he didn't even hear it. He zoomed in and asked her to look for any recognizable details on the car.

"Anything at all. A sticker, a decal, a scratch. I can run a program to dig into it." He let Sheila take the helm and showed her the controls to zoom in and out, and how to rotate the image. Sonnie stepped to the other side of the desk where Cy stood checking messages on her phone.

Sonnie nudged Cy in the arm and mouthed *Wow* while nodding toward Sheila. "She's cool though, right? She's not going to narc me out, is she?"

"As long as you're not doing anything illegal, man."

They both laughed, then looked over at Sheila.

"Do you think it's someone she knows?" Cy looked concerned and folded her arms across her chest.

"Who knows, man. But it is likely. It could be anyone. A student pissed off about a grade, someone she cut off in traffic, anyone."

"An ex-wife?" Cy rubbed her hands over her face.

"Hey. Come look at this. I think…I don't know, I could be wrong. But this dent in the passenger side door made me think of something."

"Yeah, what is it?" Sonnie leaned over Sheila's shoulder.

"Okay, so, I never saw the car, but my ex's aunt, Jacinta, had a little black car with this weird squeaky door. She hated it. When she tried to replace the panel no one had one that fit all the way.

She opted to replace the entire door, but whoever did the job didn't know what they were doing, and the door never closed properly. She eventually found a perfect fit, but the door was dented, and the color was a little off. I remember Kharla talking about it. She said the dent was in the shape of a bull with two holes at the top."

She turned to face Sonnie. "What does that look like?" Pointing at the screen, Sheila outlined with her finger what looked like the rounded top of a bull's head with horns. There were two small holes right above it.

"I'll be damned." Sonnie blew up the image, put a shadow on it, and colored the inverse image. He flipped it to a separate monitor and lightened the background. The dent was definitely in the shape of a bull. "What's the aunt's name again?"

"Jacinta, um…" Sheila closed her eyes to concentrate. "Freeman! Jacinta Freeman. But she passed away four, five years ago."

"No problem." Sonnie called up several lists, record services, and DMV records. "Who got the car when she passed?"

"I don't know. Kharla said she didn't want it. Jacinta didn't have any kids. Maybe it went to an auction or sold for parts. I don't think it even ran when she passed."

"This is going to take a couple hours to run. I'll call you when I have something."

"Sure thing." Cy reached over the desk to fist bump with Sonnie.

"Not you. I'll call Sheila." Sonnie grinned sheepishly and bit his bottom lip.

"Nah. You play too much." Cy wagged her finger at Sonnie. "Oh, will you put that protection on her laptop before we go?"

Sonnie was still grinning. He pulled a thumb drive from his pants pocket.

Sheila shifted uncomfortably. "What exactly is he putting on my computer?" The satchel was back on her shoulder, safely tucked against her side.

"Since you have the video doorbell app on your computer, it's a backdoor."

"Excuse me?"

"It's hackable, Queen. Anyone snooping around with an inkling of knowledge could put a virus on your computer." Sonnie wagged the thumb drive in the air.

Relenting, Sheila handed over the laptop. She made a mental note to learn more about apps and backdooring.

"There you go, Sweetness." Sonnie handed the laptop back after a few minutes. "Once you restart the computer, your protections will be in place."

"Sonnie, man, thanks. I'll have an ear out for your call. What do I owe you?"

He was already back in his chair. Reclining, he put his feet up on the desk and clasped his hands behind his head. "The usual, Cy. The usual."

Cy nodded as if she understood what that meant.

"Oh, hey, go out through the restaurant. Trying to keep a low profile, know what I mean?"

Sheila thanked Sonnie for his time and followed Cy to the back of the office. They were walking into the janitor's closet. Mops, buckets, and shelves of cleaning supplies lined the wall. A left at the paper towels took them to a long hallway lit up with fluorescent light.

"I don't understand how any of this is happening." Sheila was mumbling to herself, then she addressed Cy. "What's 'the usual'?"

"Open tab at the club, no cover; that sort of thing."

"Uh-huh. That's it? Nothing kinky."

"No, of course not. Sonnie is harmless. The dancers actually like him. I don't let creeps into my establishment."

They arrived at a glass door with *El Restaurante* written under a large sombrero etched on it. A server carrying a tray of tortilla chips and salsa crossed their path as soon as Sheila and Cy walked in. Tables full of patrons enjoying fajitas and sipping afternoon margaritas continued on as if two people hadn't just walked in through a secret side door.

"Where do they think we just came from?" Exasperated and somewhat annoyed, Sheila followed Cy out onto the street. Blinking and allowing her eyes to adjust took several minutes. "Cynthia..."

"It's legit. Sonnie is a little eccentric, but he's good people. Former military. He was a little too good at his job, so they severed his commitment. That and the government didn't like that he transitioned on their dime."

Sheila took all this new information in, trying to place the pieces accordingly. She still didn't understand why she'd had to traipse through an underground tunnel. "But he's a hack—"

"Entrepreneur. Sonnie is an entrepreneur. Securities and commodities."

The lack of eye contact from Cy gave Sheila the impression this conversation was coming to an end despite how many more questions she had. Later might be a better time for her to try to get answers about Sonnie so she changed the subject.

"I think...I think Kharla might have something to do with the black car." Sheila's heart sank hearing the words come out of her own mouth. A foolish part of her wanted to hold on to a little respect for Kharla, but every time she tried she ended up looking like a fool, as well as feeling like one. The car was the key to whoever was hanging around the house and Kharla had to know something about it. Sheila took Cy's hand and looked her in the eyes. "I think it's time you meet my ex-wife."

Chapter 16

The attempt Cy made to keep her feelings hidden wasn't lost on Sheila. The silence on the drive back to her house hammered it home that she wasn't so inclined to meet Kharla. When they pulled up to Sheila's house Cy took a deep breath and turned to her.

"I'm not crazy about this."

Sheila nodded her understanding. "I know. It's a lot. It's a chance to get to the bottom of this stalker nonsense though. You don't have to meet Kharla if you don't want to."

"Eh, even less crazy about you being alone with her. It's one thing when Momma Joyce and John are in the room." Cy settled back into the driver's seat. She was struggling with it, and it showed all over her face.

"Feels a little bit like you don't trust me." Sheila opened the door and stepped down from the truck.

Cy was out of the truck, walking over to Sheila's side in seconds. "It's not you I don't trust. She could be the one watching you. She's put you through enough."

"I can handle Kharlatta Alanna Murphy. Besides, Kelly is here."

Cy made a sound like her gut was inflamed.

As they walked up to the house Kelly stepped out on the porch. She wore an apron and waved at the pair with an oven mit still on her hand. "Just in time. I'm making lunch." Her excitement deflated a bit seeing their faces.

"Are you guys fighting?" Kelly set plates on the bar top. She'd made chicken bacon flatbread with frisée salad on the side.

"No." Sheila and Cy spoke in unison, then looked at each other.

"Are you having a disagreement, then?"

"Something like that."

Cy leaned across the bar with her hands clasped. "Sheila thinks we should have Kharla come over for a chat."

"That lousy cheater. Bleck. No thanks!" Kelly continued plating.

"There's more to it than that. She has information that we need."

"Or she's the one behind all this."

"What does that mean?" Kelly looked between the two of them puzzled.

The weight of it all hit Sheila once again. She hadn't even thought of how this could affect anyone she had over at the house. Telling Kelly should have been more pressing once she realized someone had possibly entered onto the property.

"Someone has been watching the house. Maybe. I don't know for sure. There's been some suspicious sightings, hence the security system. I should have told you the other night. I wanted to get to the bottom of it before I said anything to you."

They all took a break to try Kelly's flat bread in silence. Kelly didn't appear to be too concerned with the news she'd just heard, but it was clear from her wrinkled forehead she was trying to figure out how Kharla tied into it. "You think Kharla has someone spying on you?"

"Maybe."

"Well, she's shown you who she is. I wouldn't put it past her."

"Hmpf!" Cy chewed her flatbread with a *that's what I said* expression on her face.

SHEILA ON THE MEND

The cheeky little smile spreading across Kelly's face as she addressed Cy showed off her dimples. "I take it you are not keen on Kharla and Sheila having this little chit chat? You feeling insecure?"

"Kelly!"

"I'm...feeling some kind of way that's for sure. Excuse me. I need some air."

Sheila and Kelly watched as Cy walked across the living room and outside. She paced back and forth on the porch in front of the living room window.

"Sorry." Kelly turned her attention back to eating. "She's about to explode, huh? Kharla had better watch out."

"Nobody is exploding today." Sheila finished her piece of flatbread in deep thought. She plucked her phone out of her pocket and dialed before she chickened out and changed her mind. Knowing was better than not even if it ruffled a few feathers with the woman outside pacing. Cy would just have to find a way to deal.

"Kharla, it's...me, Sheila. I need you to come over."

That's all it took. Kharla said she'd be right over. It was obvious she thought *something* was going to happen between them. Sheila heard hope and a little bit of lust in her voice. Knowing she was about to dash that hope and thwart Kharla's overactive libido made Sheila feel queasy. Her efforts to dissuade Kharla, even during their separation, seemed to bolster her confidence that they would get back together. Recently she'd cornered Sheila in the pantry at Momma Joyce's under the pretense of gratitude and tried to get a hug out of her. Sheila recoiled at the memory.

Informing Cy wouldn't be as easy. Sheila joined her on the porch, thankful for a bit of fresh air herself. "Kharla is on her way over," Sheila said before realizing Cy was on the phone. She sat down on the box she kept the potting supplies in and waited with her hands between her knees.

"Okay, yeah, thanks." Cy turned around to Sheila sitting in the sunlight. "That was Sonnie. He's got a name on the car after Jacinta passed. It went to a scrapyard, then out of nowhere someone named Anna Reyes paid cash, twenty-three hundred for it. Had a tow-truck ready to take it off the lot. Sonnie is looking into where it went after that."

"Maybe that's where the parking sticker came in. Someone bought it, fixed it up, and gave it to their kid to drive to school."

"Yeah, maybe."

"Will you talk to me?" Sheila was standing again, moving toward Cy. The desire to be close was driving her crazy amidst this chaotic situation. She knew this whole thing stunk, but she could at least reassure her lover that there was nothing to worry about as far as Kharla was concerned.

Cy shoved her hands in her pockets, an attempt not to squirm or show the anxiety coursing through her body. "I don't like it." She shook her head back and forth. "This feeling in my gut is telling me something ugly is coming."

"You taking shots at my ex, sight unseen," Sheila quipped with a smirk on her face.

Sheila's silly attempt at humor had enough power to make Cy drop her shoulders in an effort to relax. They stood torso to torso for a few minutes taking in each other and the late afternoon sun before it disappeared behind a cloud.

"Come on. We'll get to the bottom of this together." Sheila led Cy back inside the house to wait for Kharla.

The sun was starting to go down when the chime of the doorbell made all three of them straighten up and pay attention.

Kelly and Cy had set up at the bar with a plate of chocolate chip cookies, cheese cubes, and slices of fruit. Kelly was showing Cy pictures of her wedding venue and dress. Sheila sat pretending to read on the couch. Her eyes passed over words, but nothing was really sticking. Once she confirmed through the camera it was Kharla she stood, adjusting her posture and breath. *In, out, in out,* she repeated to herself. Letting a beat pass before opening the door, she looked over her shoulder at the group, then opened it.

Kharla stood there grinning with a bottle of rosé and a bouquet of wildflowers from the corner store. "I'm so glad you called, Baby. I knew you'd come to your senses sooner or later." She had yet to notice Cy and Kelly as she stepped into the house.

"Don't call me baby." Sheila looked at her ex-wife with a sinking feeling. *Mistakes were made,* she thought, giving her the once over. Kharla hadn't changed physically, but the way Sheila saw her now certainly had. She was no longer mysterious and charming. Her looks hardly even registered. Now she was just a slightly below average height liar with a decent smile and a smattering of freckles across the bridge of her nose. Even her spirited afro-Dominican glow had faded in Sheila's eyes. Reluctantly, Sheila closed the door, mentally preparing herself for more lies.

The bar stool where Cy had been sitting screeched across the floor as she stood up to take off her jacket. She offered a half-ass head nod to Kharla then sat back down with her arms folded over her chest. Taking her eyes off of them was absolutely out of the question.

Kelly sat upright, biting the inside of her cheek, trying hard not to squeal.

"Oh, it's a party. I wish I'd known." Kharla made her way over to the love seat and set down her gifts.

"Don't mind them, Kharlatta. I need to talk to you about your aunt Jacinta."

"Oh, yeah? What about her?"

"Do you know what happened to that car she had with the weird, dented door?"

"No, why?"

"I've been seeing it around the house a lot. It almost feels like whoever has it is…stalking me."

Kharla sat up straight. "Jeez, bab…Sheila, that's awful. A stalker?" She sat back and began to rub her chin.

"Anything you can remember about it could help us."

"Yeah, yeah. I'm just trying to think…It was black, right? A little four door situation." Kharla yawned into her hand. Sheila saw right through that move. That's what she used to do whenever she didn't want to talk about something. Start yawning like crazy so she could excuse herself. Sheila remembered it from their fights.

"I remember the week after Jacinta's service you had to go out of town for a week. Did anyone try to call you about it?" This too was from the marriage. Sheila would counter the yawning by bombarding her with questions. Kharla's memory was inadequate compared to hers. Especially after all the lies she'd told. It was a wonder she could keep her name straight. The expression on her face usually gave her away as to whether she'd been caught, and right now she was somewhere in the middle.

"I don't remember. But it was a few years back. It's hard for me to remember anything from back then these days, Suga."

Cy interjected by clearing her throat.

"What's with security over there? Does she need a sip of milk or something?"

"Kharlatta, focus."

SHEILA ON THE MEND

She chuckled to herself before turning her attention back to Sheila. "Focus. Got it. I'm honed in." Her hands jutted out like a lane in front of her face.

"Do you know anyone named Anna Reyes?"

"Can't say that I do, Honey." Kharla was shaking her head and pushing out her bottom lip all while avoiding eye contact with Sheila.

The response was too quick. Sheila was trying to gauge whether Kharla was telling a little lie or a big lie. Either way she knew her ex-wife was indeed lying and somehow, some way she knew who was behind the wheel of her aunt's old car.

"Okay. Well, I thought it wouldn't hurt to ask. I appreciate you coming over." Sheila stood up to walk Kharla out. Cy and Kelly stood as well moving toward the living room in almost synchronized steps.

If Kharla got the hint it was time to go, she absolutely took her time getting up from the love seat. Before she reached the door she spun around almost stepping on Sheila's toes and offered to stay over. "I could help keep an eye on things." She looked up at Sheila and licked her lips.

"That's it..." Cy advanced like one of the security at her club about to toss someone out on their ass until Sheila ushered Kharla quickly to the door.

As soon as the front door was closed and locked Kelly excitedly started her assessment of the sit down. Bouncing on the balls of her feet she could hardly contain her energy. "Hoo, hoo, hooo! Omg! That was so hot! Cy, when you were all like, 'That's it!' and lunged toward her, I thought you were going to pick her up and toss her over your head or something!" She snickered behind her fidgety hands. "But before that when you stood up and took off your jacket...hubba, hubba...I bet she was quaking in her boots. That was amazing!" Her rambling recount took her back and forth across the living room.

"Can I see you for a minute?" It wasn't a request. Sheila had already walked toward the bedroom expecting Cy to follow.

"Look, I'm not proud of my—"

"What were you going to do? Beat her up?" The disappointment in her eyes lasered in on Cy's face before she closed her eyes and rubbed her forehead.

"I'm not into that macho, defend your woman crap. I told you I could handle Kharlatta." Her mouth was saying one thing while her hands were saying another. Sheila had slipped her fingers underneath Cy's shirt and scratched her nails back and forth across her stomach, then around to her back.

"What's happening right now?" Cy asked, genuinely confused.

"My mind is very clear on the matter, but my body is...a little turned on by the protective girlfriend shtick."

"Oh, okay, yeah." Cy leaned in for a kiss, but Sheila stopped her.

"I feel conflicted rewarding you with sex for that kind of behavior."

"I could...I could be talked into a spanking, maybe." The hopeful look on Cy's face disappeared as soon as Sheila snatched her hands back and crossed her arms.

Now they were both flustered and confused. They stood there eyeballing each other for a solid minute until Kelly knocked on the partially closed door.

"What are you guys doing in there? Don't leave me out here by myself. What did we decide about Kharla's involvement?"

Rejoining Kelly back in the living room, Sheila started in on her take of Kharla. "She definitely knows about the car and possibly

SHEILA ON THE MEND

who Anna Reyes is. That's going to be the key. Finding out more about this Reyes person and how it links back to Kharla."

"I think you and Kelly should come stay at mine. Now that Kharla knows we know, she might try something more."

"Okay, cool!" Kelly was all for it.

"No." Sheila shook her head and paced behind the loveseat. "We can go to my parents' house or get a hotel room. If it even comes to that. I don't think it will."

Confusion and disappointment took over Cy's features, but she didn't say anything.

"Hey, Cy, when me and Sheila go over to her brother's to get my things, will you stand in the doorway all brooding with your arms crossed, like, Hmmphf!" Kelly folded her arms over her chest and tried to make herself look bigger than she was while scowling and looking down her nose.

"Kelly..." Sheila shook her head. This wasn't the time.

"Okay, well..." Cy took a deep inhale of breath. "I guess I'll just wait to hear from Sonnie." She crossed over to the barstool and snatched her jacket up.

"Cy, don't be mad." Sheila didn't like the way Cy was acting or that this situation was even coming between them.

"But I am mad. And I'm worried...I love you too and you won't let me help."

Kelly gasped and sat up straight from her spot on the couch. Her eyes darted back and forth from Sheila to Cy.

A pit of unyielding fear opened up in Sheila's stomach and a cold sweat broke out down the center of her back. Her salivary glands were working overtime, and her throat felt like it was closed to business. "I can't...I don't...Cy. It's too..." Sheila tried to clear her throat, but it just got tighter. Her hands started to shake.

Chapter 17

Kelly jumped up from the couch after Sheila excused herself to the bathroom and Cy wanted to go after her. "Let's maybe give her a few minutes. A lot is happening right now." Kelly's smile reeked of understanding. "So, you said 'I love you' and she had a panic attack. That ever happened to you before?"

"She tried to break up with me on our trip." With hands on her head Cy stretched her back, twisting the tightness out of her body. "But then she said 'love you' the other night and I..." Cy sighed and shut her eyes. "I shouldn't have pushed it."

"The divorce did a number on her. It probably doesn't even have anything to do with you. Being a strong Black woman is exhausting. Havoc on the nervous system." Kelly was picking at the cookies and cheese from before.

Cy agreed and rejoined Kelly at the bar. "Have you heard from Bryce at all?"

"Not a peep. I should have known better falling in love with a Momma's Boy."

"Can't help who you fall in love with."

"Ain't that the truth!" They bumped a cookie and a cheese cube together in cheers. The bathroom door opened, and Sheila stepped out. There was a hint of a smile on her face, but her eyes relayed the truth. She was tired, weary, and overwhelmed.

"We can go to your place tonight. Maybe see how it feels day by day or something. I don't know." Something had changed. Still feeling uneasy, Sheila was trying. She could see how important it was for Cy to help.

"Okay, I'm okay with that."

"Well, until my new place is ready, I'm gonna need a longer confirmation." Kelly was already darting down to the basement to grab her overnight bag.

Amused by Kelly's ability to be so frank, Cy laughed. "I'm okay with that too, Kelly." Turning back to Sheila, Cy grinned a bit. "That Kelly is something else."

"Tell me about it." Sheila went to pack a few things for the night.

• • • •

"No way!" It was obvious Kelly was impressed by Cy's apartment. Every time she turned a corner, she expressed disbelief at one thing or another.

"Your bathroom is here, in between your room and the office. Linens and towels are in this closet. This door leads to the garage and gym. The gym isn't fancy, but there's a treadmill and some VR equipment if you like that kind of thing."

Kelly continued her tour down into the garage after putting her bag in the spare room. "Sheila, there's a jacuzzi down here!" Her voice carried back up the stairs as she explored.

"I really do appreciate you letting us stay."

"You're welcome. Thanks for letting me help." Cy offered Sheila a bottle of Hudson's Ginger Ale from the fridge when she grabbed a seltzer for herself.

Pleased and a little shocked, Sheila ran her thumb over the label. "I didn't think they made these anymore." She stared at the bottle. It looked almost like the original ginger ale she used to get with her dad after school at the little corner store down from her house.

"The company is still running. They downsized in the late eighties and do a lot of specialty orders for events and stuff now. I remembered you mentioned you liked them."

"I mentioned it like one time, just randomly. You went out of your way to get this for me?"

"It wasn't out of my way, Sheila. It sounded important to you, like it made you happy. That's all I wanna…" Cy stopped as the words caught in her throat. She reached across the counter and squeezed Sheila's hand. "It's been a long, emotional day. I think I'll go shower and change out of these clothes."

Kelly came back up from the garage as Cy was headed for the shower.

"Uh-oh, it feels weird in here. You two okay?"

Keeping her attention on the ginger ale bottle, Sheila confirmed everything was fine. "What'd you discover in the garage?"

"The usual. Workout stuff, storage bins, couple boxes of clothes for donation."

"Cool. Cy said help yourself to anything in the fridge and pantry. There's a little handheld vacuum for crumbs and spills under the sink. If you have questions, just ask her."

"Aye, Aye, Captain. I can't believe she lives so fabulous. Maybe I could get a job at her club and make some real money. We all know working at the realty office hasn't made me rich yet." She swirled her hips in a circle and tilted her pelvis toward Sheila. "You think I got what it takes?"

"Oh, my, well…I'm sure someone would pay top dollar for whatever that was."

Kelly let out a snort. "We should take one of those pole dancing classes. I bet Cy knows where we could find one. I hear it's a great workout."

"You'll never get me on a pole, Kelly and that's a promise."

"I bet it would free you like nothing else. I'm definitely going to look into it."

"What then?" She mumbled low under her breath. "We get free and what? We still struggle. Because we really don't know anything but the hurt." She was looking into the ginger ale bottle, searching for answers.

Kelly wasn't sure if Sheila was talking to herself or if the words were meant for her too. She stood next to the bar waiting for Sheila to explain what she meant.

"She wants to do things for me to make me happy and I should be thrilled. But in some ways it sounds like empty promises." Sheila scoffed as she looked off into the kitchen far away. "Part of me wants to believe it, but I can't. It makes me uncomfortable."

It was more than just being uncomfortable. She was afraid. *Fear,* Sheila thought. The things she'd conquered, she could make a list a mile long. Not everything in her life had worked out, but she'd amassed quite a lot, and she was rather proud of her prudent ways. But the fear, she knew, took more than it gave. It crushed parts of her spirit that wanted to soar before it could ever lift its little head.

"Let it out, Sheila. You don't have to keep going the way you're going. You can change. Like the women you study, make a new way for yourself. Subvert the system. Whatever you want."

Sheila knew Kelly was right. She didn't have to stay stuck in her current state. But it had been easier over the years to be prepared for the disappointment.

After talking with Kelly a little longer, Sheila said good night and carried herself down the hall. Cy was in her office on the phone, likely talking to someone at The Lounge or maybe even Sonnie. Sheila walked past into Cy's bedroom and grabbed her change of clothes and toothbrush to wash up before bed. The shower did her some good, but her thoughts were still bouncing from one end of the spectrum to the other, feeding the anxiety and trepidation she tried so hard to keep at bay. Once she was dressed for bed, she went in search of Cy who was still on the phone. Standing in the doorway of Cy's office, feeling maybe the most fear she'd ever felt, Sheila made a decision.

"We should be able to make the switch no problem," Cy said into the phone. The desk chair casually swiveled back and forth until she was facing the door where Sheila stood. She raised her eyebrows in acknowledgement, then tilted her head in concern. *Are you okay,* she mouthed as if sensing Sheila needed her full attention.

Afraid that if she waited even a minute longer she'd change her mind and abort the mission getting stuck in a permanent pattern of fear, Sheila motioned for Cy.

"Let's finish this later. I gotta go." Up from the chair and crossing to the doorway, Cy kept her eyes locked on Sheila.

"I..." Sheila closed her eyes and breathed out slowly. "I think I'm...I might...I need to have my hand held. I'm ready to have my hand held." It seemed like she'd been waiting her entire life to say that. A weight instantly fell away. But she didn't know what happened next.

Cy didn't say anything at first. She took Sheila's hand in hers and gave her a squeeze. "Courageous woman with the warrior spirit." She planted a kiss on top of Sheila's head. "Come on, tell me what's going in there."

In bed Sheila let Cy's warm body melt away her stress as she tried to come to terms with this new way of asking for help. It felt like an extra step she didn't particularly want to incorporate into her life. Internally she was bristling. Thinking about being needy made her skin crawl. "I don't like it."

"It's been less than ten minutes, Sweetheart." Cy nestled in close behind Sheila, taking her big spoon duties very seriously. "It's not going to be easy, but I'll help you through it."

"When you were going through it, how did you know you needed help?"

"Mmm, some of my least proudest times." Cy buried her face against Sheila's neck. "I was lying to everyone. Hiding from all my friends. Covering up bruises with makeup. Dead giveaway." Cy cringed. "I've never worn more than chapstick in my life." She sighed heavily. "The last straw was when Mom and Pop confronted me. I lost it. I had this silly notion that they would be so disappointed in me. They of course weren't."

"I hope I never run into the person who hurt you."

"Sheila, are you suggesting that you would beat her up?" Their bodies shook with laughter.

"Didn't think that would come back to haunt me so quickly." Turning to face Cy, Sheila wedged her leg in between Cy's firm thighs. "I'm not used to generous acts like the ginger ale thing. It makes me feel suspicious, sad to say."

"I understand. I really do. It leaves you waiting for the other shoe to fall. It makes you put your guard up. I know. I'll try to be more aware, but did your ex not ever just treat you, surprise you, whisk you away?"

"We did things together, but..." Sheila shrugged. "It wasn't a priority. The grad school years and then her hospitality schedule was hard on us."

"Well, in this relationship you get to decide what you want prioritized. Think about it and I'll think about it, and we can work on it together."

"It's that easy, huh?"

"No, not easy, just something that we should be willing to do for each other. I don't think it would be a bad idea for you to talk to a professional too."

"A professional? A professional what?"

"You know, a therapist, a counselor. Someone that can give you some tools to navigate things."

The way her body stiffened in response to what Cy suggested was uncontrollable. She wasn't against therapy per se. It just seemed like something other people did. Plus, when would she make time to go to therapy? "What ever happened with the thief situation at the club?"

The lines of Cy's forehead formed folds as she rumpled her face. "What made you think of that?"

"Effectively changing the subject is all."

"Ah, I see. I see. The old, 'I don't want to talk about going to therapy.'" Squeezing in closer, Cy adjusted her position next to Sheila and stifled a yawn with the back of her hand. "One of the young barbacks. She'd started using meth with some boyfriend and next thing you know things started to get out of control for her, so she started skimming."

"Damn, that's awful. What's going to happen to her?"

"She fessed up once we confronted her. She asked for help, so we sent her to rehab. The team really likes her, so we all pitched in. I hope it sticks. She works her butt off."

Sheila silently celebrated the actions of her girlfriend and the staff at The Lounge while secretly wondering if Cy embellished the part about the girl *asking* for help. Considering she was having an aversion to doing the same.

Cy yawned a couple times. "I'm fading, Sweetheart. Are you ready to turn out these lights?"

"Yeah. Let's get some rest." Sheila lay awake well after the room darkened listening to Cy's even breathing. She closed her eyes, but her thoughts didn't allow her to sleep for some time.

• • • •

In the morning Sheila struggled to wake. The muffled voices of Cy and Kelly floated in and out of her consciousness as she rolled over and buried her face in the pillow. When she rolled over again there was a bit more light and she felt slightly less groggy.

"Hey, Sleepy."

Sheila's eyes locked on to Cy as she entered the bedroom with a mug of steaming coffee in her hands. "Do you have one of those for me?"

"This is for you. Half decaf with a splash of cream, right?"

A sleepy smile spread across Sheila's face. This was one act of kindness she could get used to. "Good morning." Repositioning herself against the pillows, Sheila sat up and accepted the coffee. After a couple of sips, she felt like she was waking up.

"Kelly left for work. She asked about pole dancing classes."

"Of course she did."

"Would you like breakfast? I can make you something."

"No. This is fine," she said, sipping from the mug.

"I'll make you some eggs and toast." Cy didn't take no for an answer and left Sheila in bed to finish waking up.

"I think I'm going to sleep at my place tonight," Sheila said, entering the kitchen area.

Cy placed a plate of fluffy eggs, toast, and sliced fruit in front of her on the counter without commentary. She tossed a handful of blueberries in her mouth.

"Looks good." The fork sank into the eggs like a cloud. She chewed, aware that Cy was looking at her, but not trying to convince her to spend the night again. *That's suspicious,* she thought, but that all disappeared from her mind once the flavor of creamy, spicy, chive infused eggs registered on her tongue. "Oh, damn. That is good. Really good." She piled a heap of eggs onto the toast and took a bite.

"Glad you like 'em. It's my special breakfast for women who ask for help."

Sheila rolled her eyes, but kept eating, doing a little child-like dance from the waist up as she cleaned her plate. "What kind of plans do you have for today?"

"I need to go to the bank, then I have to get someone over to the club to fix an emergency exit because apparently a guest kicked the door last night and pulled it off the track, and Pop wanted me to stop by for lunch."

"That reminds me I need to call my father as well. I want to make sure he's alright in the house all by himself. He says he is, but, hmm, I don't know."

"One time my mom went on a three-day trip with the Rose Garden Club. I came home to my pop asleep on the couch in his boxers, cheese wiz in his beard, and their wedding picture under his arm."

"Oh, yikes. Maybe I should go over there instead of calling. He might really be in despair."

"Mmhm. Be prepared."

"You know I figured you'd meet my folks at Kelly's wedding, but now that's off, maybe you could meet my dad over dinner sometime."

Cy cocked her head to the side in surprise. "Let's make it happen." A quick look at the clock on the stove motivated Cy to put the berries down. "I have to get going. You're welcome to stay as long as you want, or I can drop you off at yours. Whatever you like."

"I'm very tempted to stay and snoop through your sock drawer, but lucky for you I too have things to do. Will you drop me off?"

"Of course. And for future reference the good stuff is in the false bottom."

Chapter 18

The front hedges looked mathematically precise and level. Samson must've recently paid a visit with his trimmer. Gliding up the front walk, Sheila realized he must've still been there. Leaves and trimmings were still scattered on the ground. She looked around but didn't see his truck. It wasn't like Sam to leave the yard in such disarray when he trimmed the bushes at the house. She used her key to let herself in the front door like she always did.

"Dad, I think we need to have a talk with Samson. He left the trimmings everywhere." Sheila made her way through the entry and kitchen, and still no dad. But the noisy laughter coming from the living room gave her a good sense he was in there.

"Dad, did you not hear me come in?"

Braxton sat on the edge of the couch, slapping his thigh and bellowing at the top of his lungs. But he wasn't alone. Samson sat opposite him in Marianne's usual spot laughing alongside him.

"What in the world is going on here?" Sheila stood just at the edge of the carpet with her arms folded over her chest waiting for someone to acknowledge her. It took quite a few minutes for the ruckus to subside. But when it did Braxton was the first to greet his daughter.

"Honey! You missed it. Samson just told the funniest joke. I can hardly breathe." He wiped tears from his eyes. He'd been laughing so hard.

"Hi, Samson. Good to see you."

"Sheila, your dad is a hoot. I can't believe after all these years we've finally sat down to catch up."

"Well, that would be Marianne's doing. She didn't like fraternizing with service folks. I told her Sam here is good people. She never wanted to hear it."

Ah, Sheila thought, *he's making friends without Marianne. How cute.* "Mom's a tough one, that's for sure." Sheila sat down at the end of the couch next to her dad. She noticed how the energy in the room was so joyous and flowing, not dry and tense. "So, what's this joke that's so funny? It's not dirty humor, is it?"

"No, no. Just good clean dad humor. You want to hear it?" Samson asked, his eyes all big and eager. It was clear he wanted to tell it again.

"Let it rip," Sheila encouraged.

Samson launched into his opening, setting up the joke while Braxton started laughing again under his breath. Once he got to the punchline Sheila was so caught off guard her bark of laughter made her lurch forward into the same position as Braxton.

They were all doubled over howling with laughter. Once she'd calmed back down a bit Sheila dug in her pockets for a tissue. She'd laughed so hard she made her nose run.

"What did I tell you? Funny," Braxton repeated.

"Brax, let me get outta your hair and go get those trimmings swept up. Thanks for the water." He took his glass back into the kitchen. "I'll see you Sunday for golf."

"Golf? Sunday?" Sheila turned to her dad, almost impressed. "And here I was thinking I needed to come make sure you're upright and dressed."

"I told you your old man was doing fine. It was a little hard at first with your mom gone over to your brother's, but it's been nice too. Seeing parts of my younger self again. I laugh more."

"That's great. How's Bryce doing? He hasn't called Kelly once to talk. I'm kind of surprised. I thought he really cared for her."

"I think Marianne is probably keeping him busy running her around town and what not. This isn't the first girl she's run off, you know."

Sheila twisted her torso sharply toward her dad to concentrate on this tidbit of gossip. "Do go on."

"When you were away at college the first time, Bryce was seeing a nice young lady, uh, Sabrina Johnston. Her folks run the thrift store across town. Well, Marianne caught them smooched up on each other in the backseat of the Mercury one evening in the driveway and she blew her top."

Absolutely engrossed by the story, Sheila inhaled and hitched her leg up under her not wanting to miss a single detail. Bryce had never really talked about his girlfriends with Sheila. Now she kinda knew why.

"Marianne dragged Bryce out of the car, fussing and a hollerin'. That's when I came outside. She told Sabrina to go get a switch! She was gonna try to whoop the girl."

"No!" Sheila let out a half chortle, half whoop of a sound and let her mouth fall open.

"Oh, yeah. Sabrina never talked to Bryce again after that. But she let everyone know what Marianne had done. He was so embarrassed. For weeks he moped around the house."

Sheila could do nothing but shake her head back and forth. Her firsthand knowledge of Marianne's tantrums qualified her dad's story, but it surprised her that she had treated Bryce to one. For a brief second she wondered again if Bryce knew Marianne had stepped out on their dad and what her character was truly like. She shook her head again to erase the thought. It didn't matter. Seemed like he'd chosen his woman and was forsaking all others.

"How have you been?"

The question sobered Sheila up from the loud laughing and gossip. She noticed how her dad folded his arms over his chest and leaned back into the couch. *Definitely get that from him.*

"I've been okay. Working on my research project, visiting with Momma Joyce when I can."

"Hmm. She getting any better?"

"Some. Her heart is weak. Kharla is a wreck over her."

Braxton rocked his whole body when he nodded. "Are you still seeing your new lady friend?"

Sheila smiled coyly. "Yeah, I am. I'm still seeing Cy."

"Okay. Good, good. When do I get to meet her?"

Sheila grinned and patted her dad on the thigh. "Soon, old man. Soon. I'll bring her by for dinner. Ooh, she can cook."

"Aww, sookie, now. That's what I'm talking about." They fell into another chorus of laughter and talked about food for a little while until Braxton had to run to the hardware store.

After the visit to her dad's, Sheila decided to make the rounds while she was out. Taking groceries over to John and Momma Joyce before she went to the library for the day would keep her from lingering well into the evening and running into Kharla. She'd been avoiding going over there after getting back from New York. The problems she had with Kharla needn't spillover into her conversations with Joyce and John. They'd want to help and that wasn't something Sheila wanted to involve them in. She doubted Kharla had been forthcoming about her affair.

She approached the Murphy's house from a side street instead of the main road out front because of the road work taking place.

Two city trucks blocked most of the roadway, dropping down traffic cones around some potholes the people in the neighborhood had been complaining about since the nineties. There were a couple of workers marking the areas where some excavating was to be done with bright orange spray paint.

Kharla was outside pacing and gesturing toward someone. *Who are you talking to?* Sheila couldn't quite see beyond the overgrown hydrangea bush Joyce kept out front, but they were clearly having a heated back and forth. She rolled down the passenger side window in hopes of hearing what they were saying, but the wind made it difficult to fully hear. Sheila sat and watched. Kharla's body language made her look aggressive and menacing as she lurched and pointed her finger at the person opposite her.

Wanting to stay out of sight, Sheila backed down the street and lined her car up with the side of the Murphy's house. Kharla was out of view, but Sheila was finally able to see who she'd been talking to. *There you are.* Sheila squinted to get a good look. It was a younger looking woman, a brunette with dark features and eyeglasses. She didn't wear any makeup or fancy accessories either, just yoga pants and sneakers.

It looked to Sheila like the woman had had just about enough of Kharla's fussing. She started gesturing and pointing back at Kharla with nearly the same intensity. The stiff, half curled way she held her mouth while talking made her look like someone who wouldn't back down no matter what Kharla was saying.

The woman turned toward the street stepping like she couldn't wait to get away from here. Kharla didn't follow. Sheila eased her car back up the side street, still watching. She wanted to know who this woman was. Every fiber in her being shouted *Anna Reyes*. There was no doubt in her mind that after she'd talked to Kharla, her ex-wife had gotten in touch with the mystery woman to either warn or scold her. From the end of the street Sheila could see her getting into a red two-door coupe. *Switch cars all you want Anna Reyes. I know it's you.* Sheila fumbled with her phone, trying to snap a pic of the woman and the license plate. She snapped picture after picture, hoping to get a couple of good clear ones she could share with Sonnie to get a definitive identification on this woman.

As Anna Reyes pulled away from the curb and navigated toward the stop sign, Sheila gripped her steering wheel, struggling to make a decision. *What are you doing, Sheila? You can't follow her. That would be crazy.* She watched the red car get further down the street. If she wanted answers, she had to act. *Follow her.*

Gut instincts and adrenaline took control, pushing Sheila into action. Her foot tapped on the gas. The car lurched forward. Avoiding the traffic cones, she maneuvered around a parked car on the street and sped to keep sight of Anna until one of the city trucks cut her off, forcing her to slam on the breaks.

"No! No! Dammit!" Sheila punched the car horn. The truck moved, but the red car was already gone. She slumped back into the driver's seat partially aware the city workers were all staring at her. Sheila pulled the car forward and parked at the corner out of the way. What had she been prepared to do? "Oh my god! Now you're becoming a stalker too." She buried her face in her hands, frustrated by her sudden lack of impulse control.

The pictures on her phone at least came out clear and crisp. Sonnie would surely be able to put a name to the face and find some answers, if only to keep her from further erratic behavior. She sent the pictures to Cy in a text.

Can you share these w/Sonnie? Need to I.D. ??Anna Reyes??

Only a few minutes passed before Sheila's phone rang.

"Baby, where are you?" Cy's voice sounded low and muffled, like she was whispering, trying not to draw attention to herself.

"Uhh..." Sheila hesitated at the four way stop then drove through the small intersection. "I'm leaving Joyce and John's." As soon as she said it she remembered the groceries in the back.

"Who is this woman you sent me?"

"I think it's Anna Reyes. Why are you whispering? Where are you?"

"At the club. We got a surprise inspection from the city. Why are you taking pictures of random women? What makes you think this is Reyes?"

"It's a long story. Can Sonnie run an image searchy thing and find out if it's her?"

"If she's online at all he'll be able to find her."

"And run the license plate too. I need to know everything."

"Sheila?"

"It's fine. I'm fine. I'm on my way home. I need to put some groceries away. Everything is okay, I promise." She could hear Cy breathing through the phone.

"I'll let you know what Sonnie finds."

The call ended before Sheila could say more. Not knowing what Cy was thinking made the hairs on the back of her neck stand up. The last thing she wanted was to have tension between them again. There was so much already swirling in and around her. Thank goodness she hadn't mentioned almost following the woman. It would have earned her a lecture for sure.

Sheila kept to the side streets on her return trip home. She felt off and needed extra time in the car to calm herself down. There was hardly anyone parked on the street when she got home. It being a weekday, this was fairly normal. But there was something in the air. A feeling of electricity, static that made Sheila really look up and down the street. She didn't like it. What Cy had said the night she met Kharla, that *Something ugly was coming*, felt real now. Something was definitely on the horizon.

Inside, Sheila reset the alarm, checked all the rooms, then took her laptop straight to the couch. Information from Sonnie could take an hour or several days. That man and his methods were a mystery to Sheila. She wanted to know something now. The pictures on her phone would have to give her something. The Mill-Amherst network connected immediately once she logged in. With the directory opened she started typing. The first search was of course for Anna Reyes. If she'd stepped foot on campus in the last six years, there might be a photo or blurb about her.

Thirty minutes into her search, Sheila did find an article about the 2014 inductees of Phi Alpha Theta. There was a grainy photo of the group with a generic caption, no names. A young woman in the second row could have been Anna, but Sheila couldn't tell for sure. She looked at the image from today. *Who are you to my ex-wife, huh?* Sheila sat staring at the photo, not wanting the obvious answer in the back of her mind to fully develop, but she knew it had to be the connection. Anna Reyes was Kharla's affair partner. Was part of the reason Sheila was divorced staring back at her? And if so, why was she coming after Sheila?

A bang of thunder crackled outside followed by the pelting sound of rain against the windows. So many thoughts from before the separation started swirling in Sheila's head. She focused on the times Kharla had been away on business. But there wasn't any one particular time that stood out. The more she tried to remember the more upset she felt. The fighting, the yelling, the lies all echoed in her head.

Sheila clenched and unclenched her hands while her vision shifted in and out of focus. She closed her eyes and lay back against the couch, trying to calm herself down, but that only made the room spin faster. "No, no, no..." Rising from the couch on unsteady legs she rushed to the bathroom where she dry heaved over the toilet. She stretched out on the cold tile floor staring up at the ceiling. "You're not losing it. You're fine. You're not losing it." Repeating the words seemed to help give her something to focus on even though the sense that she was already past losing control felt increasingly real.

Chapter 19

The rain had dulled to a drizzle by the time Sheila woke up. She was still on the bathroom floor, but it was now dark outside. Her head thrummed and her back ached from being on the floor so long. The rumbling of her stomach indicated she'd slept through dinner.

"Hmm," she shifted onto her knees and stood up using the wall for balance. In front of the mirror, she assessed the damage. The right side of her face held a faint imprint of the diamond shaped floor tile, and her eyes were bloodshot from all the dry heaving. Sheila splashed water on her face then stood leaning against the sink trying to make sense of these little attacks she kept having. They were more than just hot flashes; she knew that much. Since when did her thinking too much send her spiraling and shaking so violently?

Sheila made her way into the living room, then quickly over to the kitchen for something bubbly to help settle her stomach and maybe something to eat. When she bent down looking into the open fridge the faint sound of a car alarm going off caught her attention. A wave of uneasiness washed over her as she looked toward the door. Something told her to look out the window.

The blinking lights on the SUV lit up the wet pavement with each flash. Broken glass shimmered like diamonds up and down the road. The only window not completely busted out was the windshield, but it was smashed all the way across, along with the sideview mirrors. Sheila slowly strolled around her car with her hands on her head, sighing and taking in the damage.

"What did I ever do to deserve this?" She turned off the car alarm. This escalation couldn't be downplayed like the drive-bys. The police would have to be involved now. This was serious. Sheila jogged back across the street to the house. She hadn't thought to bring her phone with her. She'd need to take pictures for insurance, if they even covered this type of thing.

• • • •

"These things tend to be hard to prove, but we'll do everything we can to find the person who did this." The police response had been quick, but they were pretty laid back about the entire situation. It didn't seem to rank too high on the priority list of crimes to solve. After talking with the officers, Sheila sat down on the porch step to wait for the tow truck. Cy and the driver from Pittman's Towing arrived at almost the same time.

"I'm afraid to ask." Cy put one foot on the porch and leaned against the side rail with her hands in her pockets. She wore carnation pink trousers with a maroon pullover. Her hair was frizzy from the rain.

Sheila smiled looking up at her. "You always look so good. Put together, fresh, irresistible. I love that about you. Your presence makes things better, more beautiful."

It was obvious Cy wasn't expecting those particular words to come from Sheila, considering what she'd just experienced. Even in the low light of the night her cheeks showed a bit of a blush. "What happened?"

Sheila shrugged. "I was napping." She left out the part about being sprawled out on the bathroom floor sick to her stomach.

"Cameras pick up anything?"

"I'm sure. I haven't looked yet."

Cy gave Sheila a thorough once over, furrowing her brows. "I don't know if I like this blasé attitude."

Blasé? Not quite, Sheila thought. She was full to the brim of her own problems and there simply wasn't enough energy for this last one. Not yet anyway. "Will you take me home with you tonight?"

"You'll never have to ask me twice about that, Sweetheart."

"Handle the tow driver for me while I grab a few things?"

Cy nodded and stepped toward the street.

Sheila packed a small suitcase and grabbed her laptop. She set the alarm before stepping outside. A part of her wanted to look at the surveillance videos, but she also didn't want to think about this house, her car, or anything that led back to Dr. Sheila Hudson, ex-wife of Kharlatta Alanna Murphy, nemesis to some trollop.

• • • •

The sound of the garage door opening and Cy guiding the car inside pulled Sheila from her thoughts. She'd spaced the entire car ride to Cy's apartment. "Do you have work stuff tonight? Do you have to go in?"

Cy slipped the key out of the ignition and opened the door. "No. Do you want to watch the latest *Rosa, Rosa!* and snack out?"

"Thought maybe we could have sex. If you're not too tired." Sheila opened her door and stepped out of the car, leaving Cy with one foot on the garage floor and one hand on the steering wheel.

"You know Kelly is upstairs." Cy climbed out of the truck and stepped quickly around the back to help Sheila with her suitcase.

"I can be quiet."

"I don't know if *I* can," Cy said, watching Sheila's rear ascend the stairs before following her inside. "Baby, are you...Baby, hold up."

Sheila walked straight back to the bedroom ignoring Cy and started undressing while humming. When she turned around Cy was in the doorway, eyes wide and lips twitching. She shut the door behind her. "I'm not complaining, but is there something I should know?"

Standing in her underwear, Sheila shrugged. "I just need..." she stepped closer, unable to finish her thought. "You have on entirely too many clothes." She lifted the hem of Cy's pullover up until she could slip out of it. The tee underneath fell to the floor next. Her fingers trailed over Cy's skin, across her breasts, up her neck until Sheila cupped the back of her head and pulled her into a kiss.

"Mmm," Cy moaned into Sheila's mouth and let her guide the dance.

She led her to the bed while helping her out of her pants and caressing her thighs. "Can I wear your harness," she asked, looking up from planting kisses across Cy's midsection.

"Uh, what?" A flash of hesitation *and* curiosity flickered in Cy's eyes.

Sheila was thinking of the crisscross leather chest harness Cy had worn on their museum date. She'd wanted to trace the path of the straps with her fingers that night. Now she wanted to know the feeling of being tethered, restrained. From the sweat beading over Cy's top lip, she was clearly thinking of a different type of harness.

"You would let me use a strap-on?" The slow, mischievous smile spreading across her face took over.

Cy shook her head and swallowed simultaneously. "You have a wild look in your eye, Sheila. I don't...I don't think you're ready for that type of responsibility."

Collapsing in a fit of laughter Sheila sprawled across Cy's lap. "I was talking about your chest harness." She laughed until Cy was laughing along with her.

"My chest harness, right, right. I knew that."

In an instant Sheila sobered, then hovered over Cy with her most serious face. "But answer the question. Would you?"

"Um, uh, well, uh..." Cy stammered her way through a response. She rubbed a hand over her face and swallowed hard. "Maybe," she said, biting her lip and raising an eyebrow.

Sheila's eyes pranced with an impish glee as she filed that *maybe* away for later. This playful confusion had changed her mood for the better. "You surprise me, Ms. Owens." They shared a long gaze before Sheila broke the spell. "Now where's that chest harness?"

"In the closet on the left. The accessories are on the middle shelf."

Sheila darted up from the bed to retrieve the harness. In the closet she took her time choosing, letting her fingers brush over the sleeves of smart looking shirts and jackets. She reached for the black harness, but a red one with many rivets and rings caught her eye. The straps crossed in several directions. She tried slipping it on but there were pieces here and there out of place.

"I think I need help," she admitted, stepping out of the closet.

"You almost got it." Cy crawled across the bed to the edge and propped up on her knees. "Take your bra off," she said, reaching for Sheila and pulling her towards the bed. Her knuckles bumped Sheila's nipples making them perk up.

"What do you like about these?" Sheila asked as Cy buckled her into the harness. The leather felt cold on her skin at first, but warmed the more she manipulated it.

"I think it looks sexy, a contrast of freedom and restraint, structure and chaos." She slipped the end of the last strap into its clasp beneath Sheila's protruding breasts. Cy lowered her head, planting an open mouth kiss between her breasts where the crossing straps formed an open triangle. "How's that feel?"

"Tight," she said, closing her eyes. "But in a good way." The smooth finish dulled some as she stroked it. Red, the color of love, stimulated her senses. In front of the mirror, she took a long look at herself. The morning walks had her looking firm and ripe. "I'm overwhelmed," she said, looking past her reflection back at Cy. "This is the perfect representation. Structured chaos. More chaos than structure right now. I feel like such a mess."

"It's okay. You can be a mess." Cy tilted her chin up once she was back within reach. "You're safe. I promise."

Sheila let out a deep sigh and climbed onto the bed. "I'm probably going to cry," she said, her voice already cracking a bit.

"I'm due a good cry myself." Cy lay back and pulled Sheila with her.

• • • •

Light tapping on the bedroom door caught Sheila's attention and she eased out of bed. She grabbed a short robe from the chair in the corner while looking over her shoulder at Cy who was stretched out, lightly snoring. They'd made love so sweetly at first, then things got a little crazy when the nibbles turned to full on biting. The back of Sheila's legs and ass cheeks probably looked like she'd been attacked by a small woodland creature.

"Kelly, hey, what's up?" Sheila slipped out of the room and shut the door so Cy could continue sleeping.

"I just wanted to check on you. I feel like I haven't seen you in a couple days."

"I know. I've been all over the place. Are you doing okay?" They walked out to the living room and sat together on the couch.

"My new place will be ready soon. Down on Quillet Street. I still have stuff at Bryce's though. I keep procrastinating going over there. Might just say screw it and buy new stuff."

"That's an option."

"So..." Kelly was trying to be sly about something. She was looking at Sheila with raised eyebrows while biting her lip.

"What? Why are you looking at me like that?" Relaxing further into the couch Sheila wrapped one arm across her stomach and propped her head up with the other.

Kelly, exasperated and flailing, squeezed Sheila's knee. "I heard you two...*celebrating*." She grinned and shimmied her shoulders.

A slight prickly heat rose up Sheila's neck, and she shifted against the couch, uncomfortable. Cy wasn't kidding about her inability to keep quiet. She was such a vocal participant. "Sorry about that. We'll try to keep it down in the future," she said, smiling to herself.

"Well, show me the ring already." Kelly reached for Sheila's left hand.

"What ring?"

Mouth agape and stunned, Kelly stammered. "Oh, no." She shrank back, trying to disappear into the couch. "When I saw Cy earlier, she had a ring out at the bar. She put it away quick. I thought she thought I was you, ya know. Obviously trying to keep it hush hush. Then when you two were in there making all those animal sounds, I thought you two were celebrating your engagement. I'm so sorry. I shouldn't have said anything."

Animal noises? Sheila narrowed her eyes, somewhat irritated at that description. Turning her thoughts back to the matter of a ring she knew nothing about, she shrugged her shoulders. "I'm nowhere near being ready to get engaged or married again." Sheila ignored the tightening vice in her stomach and tucked her legs beneath her butt. "I'm sure whatever Cy is doing with a...you know, has nothing to do with me. That's her business."

"Yeah, you're right." Kelly nodded quickly, but her wide eyes looked so hopeful. "I won't bring it up again. I shouldn't have said anything. Cy is going to kill me, isn't she? Shit."

"No, she isn't. Besides I won't say anything if you don't." Sheila locked her lips with an invisible key and tossed it over her shoulder. She didn't want to know anything about any rings, earrings, bracelets, or any other jewelry in connection with life commitments at this point. All she wanted right now was a nice pair of arms to fall into when everything else imploded around her. Someone or something comforting and non-demanding. Sheila noticed how pensive Kelly looked sitting beside her.

"This can't be easy for you either, Kells. Engagement talk, having to cancel your wedding venue."

"It royally sucks," she said, blurting it out like it had been festering inside her. "Brie has been helping me cancel things. She got my deposit back from the caterer somehow. Some of the girls want to keep their dresses. I don't know what to do about mine." She slumped and sighed.

"So, it's really over for you and Bryce? You don't think you will work it out?"

Kelly shook her head. "It's too late. Bryce would rather keep Marianne happy, and I don't want to deal with her for the rest of my life."

"I hear you. If you want me to go by the house and grab your things, I will."

"That would be great."

"Okay, I'll plan on going later this week."

"Sheila," Kelly said, looking off blankly at the brick wall, "I did have doubts that day we went to the Wedding Festival. I just didn't want to admit it, I guess." She wrapped a strand of hair around her finger.

"Better you realize it now than once you're ten, twenty years down the road."

"True. Before I wreck my body with some big-headed children."

They busted out laughing and threw themselves back against the couch cushions.

"Okay, I wasn't going to say all of that, but yeah. I guess before babies are involved is a plus as well." Sheila shook her head. The way Kelly said things sometimes caught her completely off guard in the best way.

Chapter 20

The next morning Sheila was up early while Cy slept in. She'd had to grab her laptop and set up in the living room to keep Cy's quick hands from pulling her back beneath the covers a couple of times.

Estimates for the busted-out windows on her SUV came via call and she promptly sent that over to her insurance along with pictures and the police report.

Cy shuffled out to the living room towards Sheila still half asleep with her hand outstretched. "Here, it's Sonnie," she said, offering over her cell phone. She fit herself on the couch beside Sheila, stretching out and placing her head in her lap.

"Sonnie?" Sheila put the phone on speaker. "Did you find something?" Her hands took on the task of absently detangling Cy's hair as she listened.

"I absolutely did, my luscious Queen. That is our girl, Reyes. Great pics by the way. You snapped her up. I've got her number, address, work, financials, the last time she went to the dentist, you name it."

Yes, Sheila thought. Just like that. Anna Reyes identified. Sheila tried to think about what to do next. Go to the police? She needed more evidence. "Was she there last night? At my house?"

"Doesn't look like it. The window smasher was much shorter."

"Hmm," Sheila continued stroking Cy's hair while she contemplated. "Where does she live? I want to confront her."

Cy shifted to an upright position shaking her head *no.*

"Why not," Sheila whispered to Cy, confused why she didn't want her to make contact. "Sonnie, you can send me what you have on her. Send it to my email." Sheila got up from the couch to continue the conversation in private. Cy's pouting wasn't going to deter her from finding out the truth and putting an end to the harassment.

Cy had her elbows on her knees and her head in her hands when Sheila returned to the living room.

"Here's your phone. Sonnie said he'd call you later about the other thing. What other thing?"

"Background checks for the club," Cy grumbled, head still in her hands.

Just looking at Cy, Sheila could tell something wasn't quite right. The slumped position of her shoulders, the irritable tone, and lingering in bed all morning spoke to something being off, but Sheila wasn't sure what. "You don't seem like yourself this morning. What's wrong?"

"I'm just tired." Cy straightened up, took a deep breath, and exhaled.

It was more than that, Sheila could tell. Something was definitely bothering Cy. She didn't know whether to keep at it or let her work it out for herself.

"Did you see your folks yesterday," she asked, hoping a shift in conversation would brighten the mood.

"Yeah, I did." A hint of a smile appeared briefly on her face. "Mom and Pop say hello. Pop needed help with a new router. He thinks the neighbor kid is piggybacking off their Wi-Fi. Mom just wanted to give me a couple things she's been holding on to. Some family heirlooms and what not." Cy turned her head to the side and yawned.

A ring, perhaps, Sheila thought, but pushed the idea as far away as she could. A better thought popped into her head. One that could get Cy out of her mood *and* Sheila a little facetime with Anna. "How about we get out for a bit. I'll take you to lunch and some light shopping."

"What are we shopping for? I don't really need anything."

"Actually, you do. Kelly broke your french press. She was afraid to tell you."

"Ah. I was wondering where it had gotten to." Cy rolled her eyes playfully. "I'll hop in the shower real quick."

Sheila smiled and waited for Cy to leave the room. She opened her laptop to look at the information Sonnie had sent on Reyes. On the phone he'd mentioned that she was the manager of a restaurant downtown. Grille 5150. Sheila scrolled through the email and downloaded the address onto her phone. She was going to pay Ms. Reyes a little visit. Maybe see how a little reverse stalking made her feel.

"I hope we're doing lunch first. I'm hungry," Cy called out from the bedroom. She appeared a few minutes later dressed in dark jeans and a button down. "Ready?"

"Yes." Sheila shut her laptop and stood up. "I know just the place."

Grille 5150 was in the middle of a well-developed shopping center. Sheila came here all the time. Ironic. She wondered if Kharla met Ms. Reyes here while she was off shopping for bras or towels for their house a few stores down.

"There's a Kitchen Supply Store." Cy's face lit up as she maneuvered the truck into an empty parking space. "I've been meaning to get a cocktail smoking box. I want to recreate a drink we make at the club."

"You're such a gadget girl." Sheila hitched the skirt of her dress up as she stepped down from the passenger side. "You've got that squirrely look in your eye already."

Cy snickered and took Sheila's hand. "I do like my tech, that's true."

Sheila was on the lookout for Anna as soon as they walked into the restaurant. It was lunchtime busy, servers hustling back and forth from their tables to the kitchen. A petite hostess with a perfectly rounded afro attended to them promptly and led them to a booth.

"Enjoy."

"You look really beautiful." Cy was peering at Sheila over the top edge of her menu. "You have a glow, a heat resonating right now."

Sheila pulled her attention away from the bustling around her. The way Cy's deep brown eyes seemed to be taking a snapshot of her gave her a little zap like she'd reached across the table and touched her. Sheila brushed her cheek lightly with her fingers.

"That's funny you say that. I'm burning up." She dabbed her nose with a napkin. The air around her felt so warm. Whether it was her internal temperature rising of its own accord or knowing she was likely to see her ex-wife's affair partner walking around freely, Sheila definitely felt the heat.

"I'm serious. You look so perfect." Cy turned her eyes back to the menu then shut it closed. "I'm getting the steak frites. What about you?"

Sheila hadn't even glanced at the menu. She quickly flipped it open and decided on the first thing she saw. "The grilled tuna steak salad with wasabi vinaigrette sounds delicious."

"Mmm, that does sound good." Cy slid out of the booth. "Order me an unsweet tea. I'm running to the restroom."

"Okay." Sheila was relieved to be alone at the table. Scanning the restaurant, she didn't see Anna anywhere. Maybe it was her day off. Maybe that was for the best. She hadn't thought about what she was going to say or even do if she was there.

When the server came, Sheila relayed Cy's order and hers. Before the young man walked away Sheila put on her teacher's smile.

"Is the manager in today?"

"You know Anna?" His face cracked a smile back.

"We have a mutual acquaintance. They told me about this place."

"Nice! Want me to send her out when she gets free? I'm sure she'd love to say hi."

I bet she wouldn't. "No, don't bother her. I'm sure she's busy. Thanks though."

"No problem. I'll Be right back with your drinks."

Cy made her way back to the table. Sheila couldn't quite read the expression on her face as she sat back down, though she was partially thinking of what would happen if Anna did come to their table for a quick hello. The cat would be out of the bag and she would have to explain herself.

What the hell was I thinking coming here? Sheila reached across the table and squeezed Cy's hand. So many thoughts rattled around in her head. *When did Kharla meet Anna? When did they start seeing each other? Had it even bothered her that she would be breaking my heart?*

Their server returned with beverages and a basket of toasted breadsticks for the table.

"Your food will be out in just a bit."

"Thanks." Sheila was thankful the young man didn't mention anything about Anna being the manager.

"Did you hear me, Sheila?"

Cy had been talking to her and she'd missed it completely. There was so much noise in the restaurant she couldn't keep everything separate. People laughing, low talking, silverware clanging, and the restaurant's overhead speakers pumping yacht rock all combined with her own internal noise had Sheila stretched in about forty different directions. She shut her eyes for a second just to regulate all the sounds. Breathing as inaudibly as she could, Sheila grabbed another napkin and patted her forehead. "What was that, Honey?"

"I asked what you thought about me buying the apartment next door to mine. It could be a really good investment. I could expand my current place or rent it out."

"Oh, right. That's why you had to go to the bank yesterday. Right." She tried to appear reflective and engaged. "I think it would be great."

She was saved from further conversation by the arrival of their food. The salad she'd ordered was as she'd expected, but her stomach wasn't in the mood to receive much of anything, so she picked at it, continuing to look around the restaurant and at Cy who was thoroughly enjoying her steak.

"I think my iron is low," Cy said casually. She was down to just a couple of bites of food left on her plate.

"Maybe I should've gotten steak too," Sheila mused, knowing it wouldn't have made a difference. All she wanted was a few minutes with Anna to get the answers she deserved. "Watch my purse while I go to the restroom?"

Cy nodded while spearing a piece of tuna from Sheila's salad and settling back in the booth.

The aisle that led to the bathroom split off to the left towards a small office area. Sheila kept going toward the bathroom but stopped when she saw the plaques displayed on the wall. The management team in full color. Timothy Martin, Owner; Kyrie Jones, Operations; and Anna Reyes, Manager. Sheila stepped back and instinctively looked over her shoulder back toward the dining area. Had Cy seen this and just not said anything? Making a scene wasn't really her modus operandi, but she had to have recognized Anna in this photo. Her dark glossy hair, bright eyes, and perfectly dimpled smile. It could have been the picture Sheila had taken yesterday. There was no mistaking it.

Shit! Shit! Sheila rushed into the ladies' room and started to pace back and forth in front of the sink area. *This was the absolute, most idiotic plan you've ever had in your life!*

Sheila splashed water on her face, hoping that by some act of pure oblivion Cy hadn't seen the plaques. Who really looked at things when nature called? The ugly brown and red wallpaper had made her want to shield her eyes, maybe Cy had actually done so. She ducked into one of the stalls trying to figure out a way to explain this to Cy if it all went tits up.

Once out of the stall, Sheila smoothed the front of her yellow dress and glared into the mirror. "You're a grown ass woman! You made a mistake. You're going to own it, if it comes to that." Another patron walked in as she was finishing her pep talk.

It was a long walk back to the table. She could hear her heart in her left ear, thudding like a snare drum in a marching band. For a split second she lamented the life she used to have when everything was just barely rippling on the surface, and she could pretend she didn't know what was really going on underneath it all.

"No," she wheezed as she turned the corner. There in the booth across from Cy sat Anna Reyes. Time stopped. Sheila thought about running out the emergency exit to her left, but her feet wouldn't move. She stepped out of her body and just watched as it all unfolded. Anna slid out of the booth and stood by the table ringing a napkin with her hands. Cy turned in slow motion, looking over her shoulder. Her face cold, eyes distant. She shook her head.

"I can explain." Both Sheila and Anna were talking at once. They stood only a few inches apart.

"You knew this was her restaurant." It wasn't so much a question Cy was asking, but more of a realization.

"Do you know who I am?" Sheila wrapped her arms around her stomach as if that could keep her voice neutral and low. She didn't want to make a scene, but she didn't think she had control of herself.

Anna nodded, still twisting the napkin. "You're Kharla's wife. I'm—"

"So, you were fully aware she was married, and you did it anyway." Sheila felt her voice start to tremble. She bit the inside of her cheek, not nearly finished saying what she wanted to say, but afraid she'd start crying or yelling or swinging. "How could you do that to another woman?"

"What?" Anna looked confused. She shot a quick glance at Cy then back at Sheila hoping for some clarification.

"Sheila, she's not Kharla's mistress." That word caught the attention of a few patrons who had turned towards them.

"Can we take this somewhere else?" The fake smile on Anna's face threatened to crack.

Sheila snatched her purse from the booth and made a beeline straight for the front door.

"Sheila. Sheila, wait." Cy called after her. Standing she pulled her wallet out and tossed several bills on the table. "She was supposed to pay," she quipped, pressing her lips into a frown and striding after Sheila.

Chapter 21

On the sidewalk Sheila paced, shaking her head. The breeze plucked the tears from her eyes, and she didn't bother to wipe them away.

"You're defending her!" Once Cy caught up with her, Sheila let out a tirade she'd meant for Anna, but couldn't summon at the time. "Did she bat her eyes at you and smile? Seems to be all it takes."

"Get it out." Cy's voice was icy. She raised her eyebrows and folded her arms across her chest. "Because when you're done, I'd like to tell you about yourself as well," her nostrils flared.

Before Sheila could launch into what she wanted to say the side door of the restaurant opened and Anna waved them over.

"Please let me explain," she started, looking desperate to clear the air. "I never slept with Kharla. We never did anything. I lived next door to her aunt. That's how I know her. My sister Naomi was..." Anna looked down at the ground and bit her lip. "She was the one messing around with your wife."

"Ex-wife," Cy interjected.

"Naomi has had a really hard life, and she's got issues. When Kharla ended it for good, my sister took it really hard. She thought they were gonna have some sort of fairytale kind of life. It all went off the rails when Kharla told her she couldn't move in with her."

"Off the rails is an understatement. She's riding past my house all hours of the day and night. Following me in my neighborhood. She busted all the windows in my car last night."

"I had no idea" Anna ran her fingers through her hair, sighing. "She'd been staying with me, and I had been helping her, but she disappeared months ago. When Kharla called the other day, I thought she knew where she was. So, I met with her to talk, but she went off on me. Telling me I needed to get Naomi under control."

Sheila could see how bad Anna felt and how worried she was about her sister. It had to be hard on her too, but it didn't excuse the girl's behavior. "Anna, why is she acting out towards me? I didn't do anything to her."

"You'd have to ask Kharla for sure, but Naomi thought you two were getting back together. She said you sold your old house to start over or something."

"Oh, my god. She's been watching me longer than I thought. I said that to the neighbor when I first moved in."

"Anna, do you have a picture of your sister? We are going to have to report her, you know that, right?" Cy had stepped in between Anna and Sheila. She had Anna send her sister's photo to her phone.

"She needs help. If you press charges, she'll go to jail."

"Yeah, more like prison." A flare of anger flashed over Sheila. The audacity of Anna to ask them to help her vandalizing, terrorizing sister pushed Sheila over the edge. "How did she get Jacinta's car?"

"Kharla paid me to buy it back from the junkyard. She thought if it was in her name, you would find out about them. I guess you did anyway."

"I guess I did." Sheila walked a few feet away toward the parking lot, arms still wrapped around her middle. She looked at all the cars that belonged to countless people who probably thought they knew all they needed to know about their partners, siblings, even their parents. But Sheila knew all it took was one person making a decision to cast a ripple of pain and deception out over their lives. *What the hell did it matter now,* she thought. The damage was done and somehow kept right on doing.

She walked toward the shops, peering in the windows at the displays. It was all so nicely staged for a desired effect. Sheila smirked. She'd fallen for it for years. If she allowed herself, she still could. Everything in its place meant everything was fine. If she just closed her eyes, all the pieces of her life could fall back into place.

The Kitchen Supply Store had a sale going on according to the giant green sign in the window. Sheila stepped inside, blinking while her eyes adjusted from the bright outside light to the artificial store haze.

"Welcome to Kitchen Supply! Let us know if you need help finding anything."

Sheila grabbed a hand basket and walked straight back to the barware section without fully acknowledging the cashier. She knew what she needed. She didn't need any help. Not from the cashier or anyone else.

A set of four old fashioned whiskey glasses made their way into the basket. The cocktail box smoker Cy wanted was in stock. She pulled it from the shelf and added that to her basket as well. The french presses were just a few aisles over. Sheila took a couple steps to grab one, then stopped.

Cy stood before her with the sleeves of her button down rolled up to the elbow. "We don't have to do this right now." Cy reached for her basket.

"We're already here. Might as well." It surprised Sheila how smooth her voice came out. Like the final note of a holiday song, light, melodic, resonating.

"Let's go. We need to talk about what just happened at the restaurant."

"In a minute. I want to replace your french press."

"Sheila—"

"What?" Edgy and sharp, her voice turned to steel quickly.

"It can wait."

"No. We're already here." What Sheila didn't say was that she knew as soon as they stepped out of the store the illusion would be over. That no matter how many times Cy said she could be a mess, it didn't change how awful it felt. That all she could hear in her mind was the terribly misguided words, *you're bigger than this,* when hardly anything she recognized of herself was left. Or how unbearable it was to have people see her this way.

Cy stood back, quietly watching her as she picked up several french presses, comparing them until she made up her mind.

"That's the one you're going with?" Cy asked.

"What's wrong with this one? It's a Bodum. It's nice."

Cy shrugged and raised her eyebrows. "Mine was a Zwilling, just saying." If it was an attempt to lighten the mood, Sheila wasn't biting. She kept the Bodum french press and walked toward the registers with Cy in tow.

"Ooh looks like you found some good stuff. Do you have an account with us?" Sheila shook her head, and looked at Cy who already had her membership card out.

"Ms. Owens, nice to have you with us again." The cashier scanned the card and smiled. "Your free gift options today are an apron, a spoon set, or coasters."

"I'll take the, uh, apron."

"Great choice!"

Sheila sighed as the cashier finished scanning. Her cheerful attitude was grating on her nerves.

"The receipt is in your bag. Hope you both have a great day."

"You too." Cy walked ahead and held the door open for Sheila. "Let's go, Slowpoke."

Sheila made a series of sounds and rolled her eyes as she passed through the door.

"It may come as a shock to you, but I'm furious right now. No amount of huffing and puffing or rolling your eyes is going to get you out of this conversation."

Sheila thought Cy sounded like her dad used to when she did something that needed reprimanding as a kid. The internal tantrum Sheila was having would have been a shock to Cy if she could see it, but Sheila held herself together.

"I don't want to do this."

"Too bad." Cy took the bag and stashed it behind the passenger seat once they got to the car. "Too bad. Too very bad for you." She opened the door for Sheila but wouldn't let her get in yet. Her eye contact was locked on like a missile when she placed her hands on Sheila's hips. "This. Sucks. It absolutely sucks. I'm sorry. I really am. But how you got me here today..." Cy slowly shook her head from side to side. "That does not sit right with me. And trust me, I know this has Sonnie's stank all over it. But you omitted like a mofo today and I would like to at least know why, and I would like an apology."

"I don't like your tone, Cynthia Erin Owens." Sheila said it to Cy's profile as she'd started to walk away to the driver's side.

Cy spun back, clasping her hands together. "I don't like being a pawn. Get in the car."

Sheila scrunched her lips up under her nose, but she got in the car. After so many calm understanding responses Sheila thought maybe she'd finally hit a nerve with Cy. The glimmer of controlled anger would have been sexy if it hadn't been directed at her. Cy was right though. She'd manipulated the situation and indeed had omitted many facts for wanting to come to this particular restaurant. She'd orchestrated the meeting with Anna and now regretted how it had blown up in her face, resurrecting memories and feelings she should have guessed she'd be ill-equipped to deal with.

"Calling me by my government name..." Cy grumbled to herself as she got in the truck. Sheila sat with her hands in her lap, taking in the smooth angles of Cy's profile, trying to think of what to say. An apology for the deceit was definitely in order, but Sheila bristled at how to start it. Instead of backing down Sheila went on the attack.

"You brought Sonnie into this. You called him."

At first her shoulders bounced up and down. Then came the sound. Cy chuckled low in her throat, like she was trying to keep it at bay. But then it overpowered her, and she let the laughter out. "You're right about that. But I've never withheld information from you. You deliberately brought us to her restaurant hoping to scope her out, get in a row, what? Things could have gone horribly worse than it did. Did you even have a plan?"

Sheila sat quietly while Cy steered them away from the shopping center. She wished she'd just apologized instead of bringing up Sonnie and being defensive. She wished a lot of things. For starters she wished Cy didn't look so delectable when she was angry. The way she shifted her jaw slowly from side to side made the vein in her neck thump like an oil pump. Adjusting her position in the passenger seat, Sheila watched Cy the entire drive home. Even though she was used to Marianne's silent treatment growing up this was different, and she couldn't tell if it was good or bad.

"I'll get my things and get out of your space." As soon as they were back at the apartment Sheila darted up the stairs. She tried to

SHEILA ON THE MEND

map out in her mind where all her belongings were for a quick grab and go. There was no sense dragging this out.

"You don't have to leave," Cy said, watching Sheila bundle her laptop charger to put in the carrying case with the laptop. "I don't want you to leave."

"It's for the best, isn't it? This is too much. For both of us. I shouldn't have dragged you into my crazy ex-wife drama."

"Sheila, what are you talking about?" Cy followed her down the hall to the bedroom, then back to the living room.

"It's just going to be a fight. It's always a fight. I don't want to fight with you."

"Well, I do." Cy slightly raised her voice.

Sheila stopped packing and looked at Cy, her brows scrunched in on themselves in confusion.

"I want to fight with you. I want *you* to fight with me. Whatever makes you want to stuff it all down. Let it go. Making decisions for the both of us so you can run off? Uh-uh. That's not how this works." Her frustration was palpable. A few deep breaths and Cy was calm again. "I want to hold you in my arms and show you it'll all be okay. We'll be okay, but we have to do the hard part first."

What is she talking about? Looking around the room, Sheila felt like she was on one of those hidden camera shows. Cy obviously didn't know what *fight* meant. Sheila cocked her hip, putting all her weight to the side. She watched Cy, challenging her to say *never mind,* or *forget it.* But she never did. Maybe *she* didn't know how to fight. Something in her brain turned on. It struck her that she could be a messy wrong mess and Cy would still want to have her around.

Sheila ran her fingers through her hair and let her hand come to rest on the back of her neck. She'd never negotiated the terms of a fight before; it could all go bust. But Cy seemed to know what she was doing. Sheila took a long time to think about it, chewing on the inside of her cheek until it hurt. "No yelling and screaming," she said.

"Agreed."

"Ice cream once we're done?"

A soft smile spread fast across Cy's face. "See. You're already getting the hang of it."

Chapter 22

After a few negotiated *fights* and several pints of ice cream throughout the week Sheila and Cy found themselves back on track, closer and more open with their feelings. The way Sheila saw things now had started to change drastically. It was a different world when your partner had a reasonable framework for arguing and making up.

Kelly had noticed their extra cozy closeness and told them as much. "Get a room, already. Some of us are single and going without."

"We can't help it. We're nesting." Cy tapped Sheila's chin then pulled her in for a kiss on the cheek.

"We're going over to my place tonight. We'll be out of sight for a few days."

"Good," Kelly said, pulling her dinner out of the oven. "Might get to masturbate in peace for once," she said, not so under her breath.

Cy looked at Sheila trying to stifle a laugh. "Kelly, I thought your place would be ready by now. What's going on?"

"The roof collapsed on the building I was moving into. So, the search is back on. I can get a motel if you want me out of here. I know you probably want your privacy back." The dejected tone of her voice would be enough to elicit sympathy from anyone.

"It's fine, really. I kinda like having you around. You're like a very weird little sister."

"Aww. thanks." Kelly smiled and took her plate to her room.

Once Kelly was out of sight Sheila planted several kisses all over Cy's face. "You are so sexy when you're being sweet. I know Kelly's been kind of down lately. What you said meant a lot to her."

"Your family is my family. Plus, she got the guy across the way to start picking up after his dog."

"Come on. They said my car would be ready at four." Sheila got up from the couch and offered Cy a hand up. She couldn't stop smiling.

"Yes, ma'am." Cy took Sheila's hand up, then grabbed her overnight bag.

• • • •

The SUV looked as good as new when they picked it up. Someone had given it a wash and a wax from what Sheila could tell. It should have taken a lot longer than it had to get it back, but both Cy and Sonnie had connections that made replacing all the windows less of a hassle. Grateful didn't begin to explain how Sheila felt. It had been hard, and expensive, going without a car. Cy had been enjoying chauffeuring her around, but Sheila knew it was a pain in the butt when she needed to pop in at the club unexpectedly and sometimes that meant leaving her stranded at the apartment.

The new glass was extra shiny. On the way home Sheila kept checking the mirrors and making sure Cy was still right behind her. It was silly, but they'd been together almost 24/7 after the restaurant fiasco and it felt weird not being beside her in the truck.

She pulled up to her house and waited for Cy to arrive. They hadn't been inside a solid ten minutes before someone was knocking on the door.

"I got it." Cy immediately rolled her eyes once she opened the door.

SHEILA ON THE MEND

"Security." Kharla sighed, exasperated and annoyed. "Of course you're here." Kharla took a couple steps forward like she'd been invited in. Cy scowled and blocked the doorway.

"Stubs, what brings you here?"

"I need to speak to Sheila, if you must know. Now move."

"Sorry, you gotta be at least this tall." Cy held her hand level to her chest and laughed. "Get lost."

"Who was at the door?" The look on Sheila's face was a mix of nausea and constipation when she saw Kharla trying to get past Cy's wide stance.

"Sheila, can we talk?"

"No. Please don't come to my home again, Kharla."

Despite Sheila's response Kharla tried to shimmy in between Cy and the door. "I know you know about Naomi. She's dangerous. She's gone crazy."

"That tends to happen to women who date you." Sheila didn't miss a beat. She even laughed at herself. What Kharla had put her through had definitely pushed her over to the other side.

Kharla tried to push past Cy again, but this time Cy pushed back. She removed Kharla from the doorway easily, guiding her several steps back onto the porch. "I like a fair fight, so I can get on my knees and whoop you or you can take a hint and get lost."

Sheila stood back quietly. She had no intention of getting in the way of Cy and Kharla this time.

"Just check your car for a tracker. She did it to me. Busted out my back window and put it behind the seat. She's dangerous. She hurt Anna. I'm just trying to warn you, Sheila, Baby. I'm sorry."

Listening to her ex-wife's ramblings, Sheila realized she couldn't continue living in this house. Everything about it led back to Kharla. One little choice that she'd made over a year ago kept coming back to haunt Sheila, threatening her ability to move on. She had to make some life-changing choices of her own now.

"I made sure she left." Cy said, locking the door. "I didn't plan on putting my hands on her, but I did and I know you don't like that but—"

Sheila crossed the room and threw her arms around Cy's neck. A mix of anxiety, relief, and frustration all had her trembling, but she knew she'd eventually be alright. She also knew Cy would be a big part of that.

"Baby, you're shaking. Come sit down," Cy said. She led Sheila over to the couch, keeping her nestled in close against her.

"I'm okay." She clasped her hands in an attempt to stop the tremors. "I don't know why I'm shaking so hard." A couple of deep breaths helped settle her nerves. "I think I want to move," she said, nodding. "There's a woman after me and the way Kharla keeps popping up..." She shook her head dismissing the thought of her ex-wife lest she show up again.

"Hmm." Cy lightly kissed the side of Sheila's face and stroked her arm. "I..." she closed her mouth before finishing her thought.

"What? Am I being too sensitive?"

"No. I was going to offer you the apartment next door. I know you're probably not ready to live together full-time, but you could be close by. You and Kelly can move in a couple weeks once I close."

Sheila sat up a bit to look at Cy. "Can I think about it?"

"Of course."

Sitting back in the cradle of Cy's arm, Sheila let the warm feeling spreading across her chest settle in deep. She already knew she wanted to say yes, but she would take some time to think about it.

SHEILA ON THE MEND

"You know what we should do tonight? Make our signature cozy nest like we did at the hotel, veg out, and binge watch as many *Rosa, Rosa!* episodes as we can."

"I'll whip us up something to eat. I'm getting hungry."

Sheila glanced over at the kitchen and frowned.

"Right. You don't have any groceries." Cy laughed. "I'll run and get us something."

"You love me. No take backs."

"You're absolutely correct about that." Standing over Sheila, Cy leaned down and kissed her forehead. "I'll be back. Get us set up for maximum binge."

Sheila closed the blinds and pulled the curtains shut in the living room after Cy went out for their evening cuisine. Darting around the house, Sheila grabbed extra pillows and blankets to cozy up the couch and then she remembered how much Cy liked warm socks straight from the dryer. With a pair in each hand, one for both of them, she skipped down to the basement to pop them in for a few minutes before Cy returned. It was a small thing, but she knew it would be a nice surprise.

The smell of detergent hit her nose as soon as she opened the basement door. It was probably that damn wobbly shelf again. It wasn't sturdy enough to hold more than a gallon of anything. Sheila flicked the light switch by the stairs, but the bulb only flickered for a second. "This old house, I guess," she said, taking her time to not trip down the stairs in the dark. Once she reached the bottom, she made her way to the dryer by the pale stream of light peeking in from the window while her eyes adjusted. She tossed the socks in the dryer and felt around for the knob before turning it on. There was a bin of flashlights and random tools in the corner. If she could find her way to them, she'd swap out the light bulb.

But something caught her attention before she could get to the bin. The subtle flapping of the weather stripping she'd fixed weeks ago lightly hitting the concrete beneath the window. It made a wet *pat, pat, pat* sound. That window had been opened recently. *Fuck,* Sheila thought. The hairs on her arms and the back of her neck shot straight up while her stomach dipped in waves. She turned slowly, fully prepared to run to the staircase, but it was too late.

A shadow in the far corner moved. Sheila held her breath, trying to think, but one of her biggest fears was coming true in real time. An intruder hiding in the basement, lurking in the shadows, waiting for the opportunity to attack was front and center before her.

"I-I just wanna talk, Sheila." Naomi's small, shaky voice surprised Sheila. She sounded so young and sad, like she'd been crying. Sheila could relate. There was no malice in those first few words, but she also knew she couldn't trust anything this young woman would say.

"Okay, let's talk." The fear in her voice was apparent. Sheila didn't try to hide it. She was trying to remember her staff training for distraught students, but this was certainly more than a bad grade or roommate issues. "Tell me your name, so I know who I'm talking with." In the off chance it wasn't Naomi and a second of Kharla's mistresses had shimmied through the basement window, Sheila wanted to know who to tell the police to charge.

"You know who I am! Kharla told you!" The sudden outburst made Sheila flinch. Stepping back, she knocked into a stack of plastic totes filled with ornaments.

"Oh, you're Kharla's girl. So nice to finally meet you, N-Naomi. She has told me so much about you." Sheila took a small step toward the stairs.

"We're going to live together. But she's still hung up on you." Naomi stepped forward into what little light there was from the window. Tears stained her cheeks; her eyes were bloodshot and focused just past Sheila.

"She doesn't want me. She wants you." Sheila's voice cracked. Another second down in the basement with Naomi and she'd lose what little control she had left. She ran for the stairs, tripped on the first step, but crawled upward toward the door. The sound of her pulse thumping in her ears drove her to keep going. *Go, go, go,* she chanted to herself, trying to keep her footing. From the landing she pulled herself up with the handrail and cut herself on a nail. The stinging pain didn't make her slow down, but Naomi grabbed her ankle, pulling her down on all fours.

"No!" Sheila kicked out, freeing herself from Naomi's grasp and launched herself into the kitchen, banging her face into the floor as she scrambled to get up.

"Just let us be together, Sheila." The soft, sad voice had disappeared. Naomi stepped into the kitchen after her and looked around. "If you give her the house, we can finally move in together." She rubbed her flat palm across the countertops, still advancing, but slowly. "This isn't the same kitchen from before," she mumbled to herself, looking out the small window, then back toward the basement.

It made Sheila sick to think this young woman had been in the house she'd shared with Kharla, but she wasn't surprised. Not much else could shock her right now. Dizzy still from hitting the floor, Sheila stumbled forward again. She couldn't get her feet solidly under her. The only thing on her mind was getting out of the house when she heard the sound of a knife leaving the butcher block. The tinny scrape of metal made her scream. Looking over her shoulder as she scrambled was a mistake.

"Naomi, let's just talk! You don't have to do this!" Any reserved calm Sheila had left was gone. She fell into a rambling flux of words that didn't seem to be getting through to the girl as she continued to advance with the tip of the knife pressed against her thigh.

"Let her love me, Sheila!" She raised the knife and lunged at Sheila as she hurriedly crawled across the living room floor.

Cy came through the front door with a giant grin on her face and a bag of groceries in one arm. A small stuffed bear sat on top peeking out over the edge. "Who's the best girlfriend in the world?"

"No!" Sheila's scream filled the air. She scurried back towards the wall as Naomi brought the knife down, slashing her thigh. Naomi raised the knife again.

Cy dropped the groceries, springing into action. She threw the bear at Naomi. With all her strength, Cy reached for the hand wielding the knife, then pushed Naomi back a few steps, slamming her wrist into the back of the loveseat until she dropped the blade.

"Sheila! Sheila!" Naomi cried, wilting to the floor once she no longer had control of the knife. Her wailing noises rang through the air as Cy held her to the floor. It brought tears to Sheila's eyes listening to the heartache rippling out of her. It was so familiar and took her back to the early days of her divorce. She'd been out of her mind from pain too.

• • • •

Even though she'd just experienced the terrifying ordeal firsthand, it was already hazy in her mind, what had happened. It was like a bad dream dissipating. She watched Cy give her statement to the police as the paramedics dressed her wounds and gave care instructions, though she heard almost none of it. However, she was painfully aware of sitting on the coffee table with her jeans down by her ankles with strangers milling about.

"Definitely selling this house." Sheila stood up, sliding her jeans up over the bandages on her thigh. A weary upturn of her lips opened up her face as Cy approached and the police and paramedics left. The deep sigh she let out inspired Cy to grab her and pull her close.

"I don't know what to say."

"I do," Sheila said, looking up. "Your timing is beyond impeccable."

Chapter 23

A month later Sheila sat with her legs crossed, waiting comfortably in the corner, mindlessly fingering the scar on her thigh through her dress while Cy walked in and out of the closet. Each time she swapped out a blazer or shirt or pair of pants trying to find the perfect combination.

"What was wrong with the green?"

"Too tight across my stomach. I don't want to pop a button at dinner and put someone's eye out." She stepped out and posed in front of the mirror. This time she was wearing all gray with a yellow pocket square. "Yes? No? Maybe?"

Sheila frowned and shook her head. "The navy was nice."

"Ugh," Cy made a sound like she was unsure. Her frustration was showing through. "I look like I'm going for an interview."

The stifled chuckle from the corner still made it to Cy's ears. Sheila couldn't help it. Cy was cute when flustered. "Braxton Hudson isn't going to care what you're wearing. He's just glad that you make me happy. He loves you already, like the daughter he never had."

"Ha, ha! Very funny." Cy flipped up the collar of her shirt, then flipped it back down. "I want to make a good impression."

"You will." Sheila crossed the room and stepped into the closet next to Cy. She grabbed a crisp, white shirt and navy pants and handed them to her.

"You sure?" Cy held the clothes up to her frame.

"It's either this or you wear my dress, and I wear the pants."

Cy laughed, slipping out of her current clothes for what Sheila had picked out. "Is Kelly riding with us or meeting us there?"

"She's meeting us at my dad's." Sheila primped in the mirror, running her fingers through her hair, and checking her teeth for lipstick smudges.

"And you're sure I don't need to bring anything? I could whip up a side."

"No. I stopped at Farmington's and picked up ready-made. Roasted potatoes and the asparagus tips."

"But your dad knows I can cook though, right?" Cy struggled to feed her belt through all of the loops of her pants. She twisted her torso trying to see where she'd missed a loop and ended up spinning herself around.

"Let me help." Sheila pulled the belt all the way out and began snaking it back through each loop while encouraging Cy to breathe. "Imagine how I felt meeting your mom on our second date."

"That *was* wild, wasn't it?" Cy smiled, remembering.

"One of my top five dates of all time." Sheila smoothed down Cy's shirt collar then brushed her hands across Cy's shoulders. "Perfect." It felt nice to be reassuring Cy for a change.

Braxton's house was bright with noise when they pulled up. Kelly was already there with her soror Brie. Samson and his wife Yolanda arrived just after Sheila and Cy. They all took turns introducing themselves and how they knew each other. Sheila made sure Cy was fine being left alone for a few minutes before stepping away to the kitchen to help Braxton with the food.

"Dad, this is great!" She put the potatoes and asparagus containers down then gave him a long hug and pinched his cheek. He looked the happiest she'd ever seen. He'd let the gray at his temples flourish, and it made him look extra distinguished. His clothes fit more loosely too, and the smile on his face didn't seem to let up.

"Is that parmesan zucchini I'm smelling?"

"You bet it is. Samson and Yolanda brought peach rum pound cake and Kelly brought something too." He looked around until he spotted the large, covered aluminum tray. "There, pasta salad."

Sheila started loading up the serving carts to roll out into the dining room and let the banter from the other room wash over her. It was soothing to hear people laughing and chatting with no drama in sight. She locked the wheels on the first cart so the veggies wouldn't roll away and started setting plates around the table.

"Is this a different table?" She asked over her shoulder. Braxton had come around from the kitchen with the brisket.

"Yolanda made it. She's a master carpenter. You should ask her about her work."

"I will," she said, impressed at the detail and finish. "Hey, there's eight chairs. Is someone else joining us?"

"Uh, yeah. There is someone else joining us, actually. She's going to be a little late, but I think you'll like her."

Sheila stopped setting the table and looked her dad up and down. "Are you seeing someone?" The look on his face told it all. His eyes danced and his cheeks grew big with his smile. Sheila's mouth dropped open in surprise and joy. He absolutely deserved a healthy relationship. Marianne had stifled his spirit long enough. The separation had been good for him, really good. Now Sheila couldn't stop smiling. She snuck out of the dining room while Braxton went back to the kitchen for the chicken.

"Cy," she whispered, waving her over frantically. If she didn't tell someone, she was going to burst.

"Hey, what's up?"

"My dad has a girlfriend. She is coming here tonight."

"That's awesome!"

"Shh." Sheila giggled like a schoolgirl with a finger over her lips. "He's so happy. That makes me happy."

"And you being happy makes me happy." Cy stole a quick kiss and winked. "Do you want to tell everyone our good news tonight, too?"

Sheila's face opened up in a wide, gleaming grin. She felt her face getting warm, but she shook her head. "It's my dad's night. We can tell people some other time."

"Okay. Whenever you're ready." Cy winked again and then returned to the group.

Once the table was set and food laid out, Braxton called everyone to the dining room. The oohs and ahhs made him chuckle and beam with pride.

"This spread looks incredible," Samson said, looking up and down over the table. He was quick to sit and get comfortable.

"It sure does." Cy pulled out the chairs for Sheila, Kelly, and Brie since they were all sitting on the same side of the table.

Yolanda nudged Samson in the shoulder after seeing the show of thoughtfulness. He got back up and promptly pulled out her chair, then looked over at Cy.

"Making me look bad, Youngblood." Everyone laughed.

"No disrespect whatsoever." Cy kept up the lighthearted banter.

Sheila spoke to Yolanda across the table about the exceptional craftsmanship they were all sitting at while everyone started passing dishes and engaging in their own conversations. The crosstalk brought a lively energy to the room, something Sheila guessed hadn't been present for quite some time in the house.

Then the hum of concentrated eating took over, just the sounds of silverware hitting plates. Once everyone noticed how quiet it had gotten they all looked at each other and burst into laughter again.

"You know it's good when everyone gets quiet," Brie said, dipping her asparagus in garlic and going silent again.

"Mmhm," someone agreed.

The doorbell chimed and Braxton was quick to put his utensils down. "I'll get that."

Sheila bit her lip and tapped her toes against the floor nervously as she watched her dad cross the room. She looked at Sam and Yolanda quizzically.

"Have you two met her?"

"Who?"

"Dad's new friend?" They both shook their heads. Sheila squeezed Cy's thigh under the table. She was absolutely vibrating from anticipation.

"Everyone," Braxton stepped back into the dining room, just pausing at the entrance. "I'd like to introduce you to my special friend Gail. We met at the new bookstore."

"Oh, my goodness! Oh, my goodness!" Sheila couldn't believe her eyes. Her favorite purveyor of stationery supplies stood beside her dad, holding his hand. "Gail!" She squealed, rising from her chair.

"Sheila!" Gail released Braxton's hand and sauntered over to meet her best customer with open arms.

"You two know each other?" Kelly asked.

"They must!" The group let the excitement carry them all into another boisterous round of merriment, then started to introduce themselves individually to Gail before carrying on with the evening.

Sheila looked around the table, the only one not engaged in conversation and took it all in. Family, good friends, and good food all within reach. The feeling of joy filled her chest until she thought she might overflow. For the first time in as long as she could remember Sheila felt like a happier, healthier version of herself. It was almost more than she could bear, and she couldn't wait until tomorrow to tell her therapist all about it.

The End

Don't miss out!

Visit the website below and you can sign up to receive emails whenever Krystal A. Smith publishes a new book. There's no charge and no obligation.

https://books2read.com/r/B-A-YSUHC-BBXYE

BOOKS 2 READ

Connecting independent readers to independent writers.

About the Author

Krystal A. Smith is a poet and speculative fiction writer. Her poems have appeared in Entropy Magazine, Serendipity, Kissing Dynamite, and Sinister Wisdom. Her collection *Two Moons: Stories* was a 2019 Lambda Literary Award Finalist. Her poetry collection, *This is Not About Love* (BLF Press, 2021), explores the complexities of human emotion and relationships via memory, experience, and imagination. Follow Krystal @authorkasmith (twitter).

Milton Keynes UK
Ingram Content Group UK Ltd.
UKHW030748071024
449371UK00006B/448